Meet P[...]

Her special [...]
is laun[...]

Penny has been writing exclusively for Mills & Boon® for twenty years, from her home in Cheshire where she lives with her husband, three dogs, and two cats. Brought up in Preston, Lancashire, Penny's family moved to Cheshire when she was seventeen. She started her working life as a secretary in a bank, but had always told and written stories for herself and her family.

After reading an article in a magazine about how Mills & Boon were looking for new writers, she submitted a story just out of curiosity. With very few amendments, that first submission was published, and one hundred novels later, what started as a hobby is now a way of life.

'All my books are special at the time of writing,' says Penny, 'which means I don't have favourites. I have left it up to the editors at Mills & Boon to tell me which have been most popular, and which should go into the Collector's Edition, because what matters is what my readers like.'

Look out for this exciting 'Collector's Edition' over the coming months

MILLS & BOON

Penny Jordan

COLLECTOR'S EDITION

You Owe Me

'The tongue may lie, Catriona, but the body can't. There's only one way to satisfy the longing we both have for each other.'

Catriona looked at him in desperate, heart-thudding silence. Her hands, which up till now had been hanging helplessly by her sides, now made a feeble attempt to push Ryan away. Feeling the warmth and firmness of his flesh beneath the thin cotton shirt, she couldn't help herself, and her fingertips played over the rippling sinews and muscles of his back.

'You want me, don't you, Catriona?' he asked huskily. 'I want to hear you say it.'

Alex Ryder was born and raised in Edinburgh and is married with three sons. She took an interest in writing when, to her utter amazement, she won a national schools competition for a short essay about wild birds. She prefers writing romantic fiction because at heart she's just a big softie. She works now in close collaboration with a scruffy old one-eyed cat, who sits on the desk and yawns when she doesn't get it right, but winks when she does.

REVENGE BY SEDUCTION

BY
ALEX RYDER

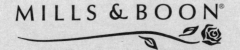

All the characters in this book have no existence outside the imagination of the author, and have no relation whatsoever to anyone bearing the same name or names. They are not even distantly inspired by any individual known or unknown to the author, and all the incidents are pure invention.

*First published in Great Britain 1998
Harlequin Mills & Boon Limited,
Eton House, 18-24 Paradise Road, Richmond, Surrey TW9 1SR*

© Alex Ryder 1998

ISBN 0 263 80822 X

*Set in Times Roman 11 on 12 pt.
01-9806-52372 C1*

*Printed and bound in Great Britain
by Mackays of Chatham PLC, Chatham*

CHAPTER ONE

CATRIONA almost choked over a mouthful of coffee when she saw the picture in the morning paper. She clattered her cup down in the saucer and tried to stifle a groan. Well, there'd be no phone call now. That was one dream which would have to go into cold storage. Feeling sick at heart, she pushed her Sunday breakfast aside.

From across the table Madge regarded her through world-weary, morning-after eyes. 'What's wrong? Another scandal in high places?'

Catriona stared at the picture again. Oh, there was no mistaking that man! Tall, broad-shouldered and immaculately dressed. A rakish tilt to the dark eyebrows and a finely chiselled nose and jawline. The same genial smile on the wide, generous mouth.

For a moment her head spun and her heart thudded as she remembered how it had felt when he'd first taken her in his arms. She shivered as she recalled the delicious, nerve tingling instant his mouth had claimed hers...and later...when those strong, sensitive fingers had slowly begun to undress her...

She got a fierce grip on her emotions and murmured, 'Nothing... It...it's nothing, Madge.'

'Huh! You're acting pretty damn strange over nothing. Let me see that.' She reached over and took the paper from her hand. After studying the picture, she read the text aloud. '''Ryan Hind, the well-known, swashbuckling property tycoon, and Miss Diane Rees-

Boulter seen last night dining at Cardini's in the West End. Diane is the latest in a seemingly unending line of attractive young ladies to be squired around the nightspots by London's most sought-after bachelor. Can we look forward to the society wedding of the year in the near future? Don't hold your breath.''

She let the paper drop, then stared at Catriona in silence before raising her eyes imploringly to the ceiling. 'Please don't tell me that you've got yourself involved with that despicable excuse for a man! He's every mother's nightmare. I should never have gone on holiday and left you on your own.' She heaved another sigh of sympathy. 'Come on then, young lady. Tell me all about it.'

It was hard to believe how much of a fool she'd been, and even harder to admit it to someone else, especially Madge, who'd looked after her like a daughter. 'I...I met him two weeks ago,' she began in a subdued voice. 'He...he was so charming...and before I knew it I'd accepted his invitation to dinner that evening.' She toyed with her cup, reluctant to go on.

'Well?' asked Madge impatiently. 'Then what happened?'

She drew a deep breath and took the plunge. 'He sent a car round here to pick me up at seven-thirty. We had a wonderful dinner. Then he...he took me to his hotel and...and we spent the night together.' She looked at Madge, her eyes pleading for understanding. 'He was so kind and...and wonderful, and he made me feel that I was the most important thing in the world to him.'

She paused and swallowed the bitter taste in her mouth. 'In the morning he was gone. There was a note on the bedside cabinet explaining that he'd had to leave early to catch the Paris plane but that he'd get in touch with me the moment he got back in a few days' time. There was also a twenty-pound note for the taxi fare home.' She swallowed once more. 'I...I really did believe that he'd keep that promise to call me when he'd returned from France. And now...' She pointed a quivering finger at the newspaper. 'There he is as large as life with...with someone else!'

Madge shrugged. 'So? Now you know the kind of creature he is. My advice to you is just to forget him. Believe me, you're well rid of that rogue. He's bad news.'

Catriona's breathing became rapid and shallow as the full realisation began to slowly sink in. All those whispered endearments...the murmured promises and declarations of undying love...nothing but empty lies!

She clenched her fists as a cold rage gripped, then pierced her heart. For a moment she was too choked to speak, then she exhaled an explosive breath. 'I'd never slept with a man until I met him! He took advantage of me and now he's dumped and humiliated me! And you expect me to forget him!' She managed to get herself under control, then laughed bitterly. 'I suppose I've got no one to blame but myself. You'd think that at twenty-one I'd have more sense, wouldn't you? Now I know what my mother meant when she warned me about coming to London.'

Madge stared at her in amazed disbelief, then reached for another aspirin, washed it down with a mouthful of black coffee, lit another cigarette, coughed harshly, and spluttered, 'Are you telling me that you were a virgin? At twenty-one! My God!

Were there no red-blooded men in that unpronounce-able Scotch village you came from?'

'Kindarroch,' she muttered. 'And the McNeils of Kindarroch never forgive nor forget an insult. If any of my kin ever find out what he's done he'll be de-prived of the means of ever doing it to another woman.'

Madge gave a shudder. 'Yes…quite… Well, it was some time back in the Jurassic age when I lost mine. He was the drummer in a rock band and I…' She paused, then smiled wryly. 'I'm turning into a boring old bag. I've told you all this before, haven't I?'

Catriona nodded indulgently. 'Yes, Madge, you have. I've heard every detail of your lurid past. No one could deny that you've led an interesting life. You should write a book about it some time.'

A scattering of ash spilled down Madge's dressing gown as she laughed shrilly. 'My dear girl, there are lots of people in this town who'd pay me a fortune simply not to write a book. But what the hell…I'm no tell-tale.' She squinted at her through a cloud of smoke. 'Mind you, I would have told you about Ryan Hind. Everyone in London knows about his reputa-tion. I've even met him at a couple of those Chelsea bun-fights. Course, he never paid any attention to an old wreck like me.'

Catriona was still finding it almost impossible to accept the truth and her blue eyes looked at Madge in misty appeal. There was always hope, wasn't there? 'Are…are you sure about him, Madge? Is he really as…as bad as you say? I find it hard to believe. He seemed so sincere.'

Madge studied her thoughtfully, then gave a sigh and said quietly, 'I'm a fool. I should have realised

straight away. You fell in love with him, didn't you?'
She saw the answering miserable nod and went on in
a slightly bemused voice, 'Good old-fashioned love
at first sight. I thought it had gone out of fashion. But
I was wrong. Now I know why you were still a virgin
at twenty-one. You're too principled to indulge in sex
for mere pleasure. You would have to be in love with
the man first. And of course you would have to believe that he was in love with you.'

Catriona felt too choked with embarrassment and
anger to answer and Madge nodded in commiseration.
'I'm afraid that your Mr Hind is every bit as black as
he's painted. There's hardly a social event in this city
where you won't find him with some ravishing young
beauty clinging to his arm. Never the same one two
nights running, mind you. And even then I've been
told you can almost see those shark-grey eyes of his
searching out his next victim. The man is a womaniser
of the worst kind. An absolute rake.' She studied
Catriona's reaction in silence, then shrugged and muttered, 'I'm only sorry that I wasn't here to warn you
about him.'

Catriona shook her head. 'You needed that short
holiday in the sun. I should have been able to look
after myself.'

'Oh, well, don't blame yourself too much,' Madge
consoled. 'I'd have probably been taken in by his lies
myself at your age. He might be the worst thing to
hit London since the Great Plague, but I must admit
that he's a handsome-looking devil.'

She studied the end of her cigarette for a moment,
then said disparagingly, 'They call him The Golden
Hind. And it isn't just because of his ability to make
money. The *Golden Hind* was Sir Francis Drake's

ship, and we all know what a freebooting pirate he was.'

She took another draw at her cigarette and drawled, 'The word around the West End these days is that he's either doing it for a bet or he simply wants to see how many women he can seduce in a year. Trying to break some sort of record, I suppose. Personally I think he should be painlessly neutered so that women can go about in safety.'

'Well, he made a mistake when he put me on his list,' muttered Catriona darkly. She retrieved the paper and looked at the picture again. The anger burned in her throat at the sight of him and she said bitterly, 'Cardini's! That's where he took me on the night it...the night it happened.'

'He takes all his victims there,' Madge said casually. 'It's his favourite restaurant. He has a table permanently booked there and Humphrey the head waiter has orders to shoot any uninvited guests on sight.'

Catriona studied the picture of the girl by his side. She was a slim blonde hanging onto his arm and gazing up at him in obvious adoration. 'I'm sure I've seen this girl before,' she said. 'Her face is vaguely familiar.'

'It should be. She's one of the current ''Chelsea set,''' Madge said disdainfully. 'They've all been in the shop at one time or another. Tailored suits and chiffon scarves. They go for the trendy female executive look, although I doubt if any of them has enough intelligence to hold down a job. When the Golden Hind dumps her, I for one won't feel sorry.'

'Well, I will,' Catriona disagreed. 'No girl deserves to be treated that way. We've all got feelings, haven't we? We are not just put here as playthings to satisfy that man's lust. He's nothing but a moral degenerate who deserves to be smitten by the hand of vengeance, and I'll be that hand if I only get half a chance.'

Madge raised delicate eyebrows. 'Hmm... Very biblical language you Scots indulge in.'

Catriona felt a little sheepish after her outburst and she gave an embarrassed smile. 'Aye. It comes from going to the kirk every Sunday and listening to the Reverend McPhee preaching fire and damnation from the pulpit. If he knew about me now he'd have me in sackcloth and ashes.'

'I was never bothered by a conscience myself,' Madge said brightly. 'No doubt there's a special place waiting for sinners like me, but in the meanwhile...' She waved a negligent hand around the room. 'I've been wise enough during my dissolute years to acquire this charming flat, a successful boutique in Chelsea and a nice little portfolio of shares for my old age. I never, ever met a man with whom I'd want to spend the rest of my life, but that never stopped me from using them for my own ends. Mind you, I never knowingly made an enemy, and most of those men and I are still good friends. I still manage to get invited to all the right places.'

Catriona regarded her with genuine affection. 'I don't care what kind of life you've led, Madge. To me you'll always be an angel. Until I met you I was desperate and ready to slink back home with my tail between my legs. Then it all changed. You gave me a decent job and even a place to live. I'll be eternally grateful to you.'

'Well, you had such an honest face,' Madge said with a grin. 'You don't see many faces like yours in London these days. In this day and age you have to learn to spot a fake at fifty yards or you get taken to the cleaners.'

'Aye…' muttered Catriona. 'Just like I did.'

'Oh, cheer up, girl! It isn't the end of the world. You've got a broken heart and the world seems empty. But you'll get over it. You're young, but you're a quick learner, and if you take my advice you'll put this behind you and get on with your life.'

Catriona lowered her eyes. She didn't want to hurt Madge's feelings but Madge just didn't understand. Where she came from such things were a matter of family honour, not to mention pride and self-respect. Ryan Hind had trampled that into the mud and one way or another he was going to pay. She didn't yet know how she was going to go about it, but she'd find a way to make that man wish he'd never laid eyes let alone a hand on her.

Seeing Madge reach for the aspirin bottle again, she eased back her chair and got to her feet. 'You were late home from that party last night and you're still a bit under the weather. I know we were going to take stock in the shop today but I can quite easily do that on my own. Why don't you just take it easy and have a day in bed?'

Madge looked at her gratefully. 'That's kind of you, dear. I'm afraid I can't handle late nights like I used to. I'll spend the day resting. But make no mistake, once my batteries are recharged I intend growing old disgracefully, so don't order a Zimmer frame yet.'

Catriona cleaned up the breakfast things first, then tidied the lounge. Satisfied with her handiwork, she took a final look round, then smiled. When Madge had offered her a spare room in her flat at a nominal rent she'd never expected anything as grand as this!

Madge had taste and style. Period furniture and luxurious carpeting throughout, and double-glazed sliding doors led from the lounge onto a balcony offering a fine view over the river.

For a moment as she gazed out towards Chelsea Bridge she felt a brief tug of nostalgia for the wild seascapes and the rugged grandeur of the mountains surrounding Kindarroch, then she took a deep breath. Only losers allowed themselves to wallow in self-pity and homesickness.

She'd almost succumbed. Her first few weeks in London had been a heartbreaking round of menial, poorly paid jobs and a hunt for half-decent accommodation, and she'd been rapidly running out of money. It had only been because of Morag's prediction that she'd meet someone who'd become a good friend that she'd stuck it out.

Of course, Morag had also said that she'd meet a rich, handsome man, but she'd neglected to tell her that he'd turn out to be a lying lecherous swine. But then perhaps she shouldn't have taken Morag too seriously in the first place. It all seemed so long ago now, and yet it was only a couple of months or so since the day she'd decided to leave Kindarroch.

There were people in Kindarroch who'd have sooner walked barefoot over broken glass than cross the threshold of Morag's cottage up on the hill, but Catriona wasn't the least bit nervous.

The older generation, even her own mother, always spoke about Morag in whispers, after looking over their shoulders to see that she was nowhere around. Morag was the seventh daughter of a seventh daughter, so no one was surprised that she had the 'gift'.

She was a seer who had visions of the future. Well, that was quite acceptable in a culture where romantic myth and legend lived comfortably alongside satellite television and microwave ovens, but it was whispered that Morag could see right into your heart and mind. Naturally enough that made folk a little wary of her, because everyone has their little secrets, and they tended to avoid her eye as much as possible.

None of this bothered Catriona. As far as she was aware old Morag had never harmed a soul in her life and that was more than could be said about most.

She'd been on her way home from the post office when she'd spotted Morag ahead of her, bent over with a bag of shopping in each hand, and she'd caught up and offered assistance. And now that they'd reached the cottage it would have been churlish not to accept Morag's invitation to come inside and have a cup of tea.

Morag removed her shawl and smiled gratefully. 'Just put the bags down, Catriona, and make yourself comfortable while I go into the kitchen.'

She made herself at ease on a chair by the scrubbed pine table and looked around the tiny living room with mild curiosity. From the window you could see right across the harbour, empty now except for a few gulls waiting patiently on the sea wall for the arrival of a fishing boat. Towards the south the dark and jagged peaks of Skye were just visible above the hazy horizon.

As for the room itself, she found it faintly puzzling at first. It was clean, with everything polished to perfection, but it was so...so old-fashioned. It was like stepping into a time warp. That heavy wooden radio, for example. Casting her eye around, she saw that everything seemed to belong to the twenties or thirties.

Then she remembered the stories about Morag. It was said that she had come from one of the islands, sailing alone out of the morning mist into the harbour, a dark-haired, softly spoken girl of seventeen. She had fallen in love with a handsome young fisherman from the village and within a month they were married.

Then tragedy had struck. Two days after the wedding her new husband's boat had been overwhelmed in a storm and all the crew had perished. Ever since that dreadful day she'd lived here by herself and it was said that she spent most of her time at the window staring out to sea awaiting the return of her lost love.

It was a story which always touched Catriona's heart, but she'd often wondered... If Morag really did have the 'gift', why hadn't she warned her husband not to sail that day? Then again, as some maintained, perhaps it had been the traumatic shock of losing him that had awakened the dormant power.

Once again she gazed around the room thoughtfully. Was this exactly how the place had looked when Morag had first set up her new home? Nothing added...nothing taken away...nothing changed from that day to this. Everything preserved and lovingly cared for. A shrine, in fact?

Suddenly she remembered something else. She'd been about eight years old at the time and a crowd of them had been playing down by the harbour. Jamie Reid had made a catapult and he was using the sea-gulls as target practice when Morag had descended on them.

'Jamie Reid...' she'd said in a soft, sorrowful

voice. 'Don't you know that every seagull has the soul of a drowned sailor awaiting to be born again?'

It wasn't the sort of thing eight-year-old kids thought about, but she'd never seen Jamie playing with that catapult again.

She stopped her reminiscing and got to her feet as Morag came through from the kitchen bearing a tray. 'Is there anything I can do to help?' she asked politely.

Morag smiled. 'You've helped enough as it is. I'm still not too old to look after a guest.'

She smiled back and watched in silence as Morag poured two cups of tea. The knuckles on the crooked hands looked swollen and arthritic and she wondered just how old Morag really was. She had to be seventy-five at least. Her face was wrinkled, and yet in spite of her apparent frailty you could feel the inner strength and vibrant energy of the woman.

'Well, now...' Morag said, lowering herself carefully into a chair opposite. 'It's a while since I've seen you, Catriona. You're quite the young lady now. Twenty-one, isn't it?'

'Aye. A month ago.'

Morag nodded and smiled. 'You always were a pretty girl, but you're even prettier now that you're a woman. You've the sky-blue eyes of your mother and the red hair of your father. A McNeil if ever I saw one. And how are they both keeping, these days?'

'Och, they're fine enough, Morag. Like everyone else up here they're just waiting for the fishing to get better so that folk have a bit of money in their pockets.'

'Aye...' Morag sighed and looked towards the window. 'Times are hard, right enough. I dare say they'll be a bit upset at first when you tell them you're leaving.'

Catriona's cup stopped halfway to her mouth and she blinked in astonishment. She hadn't confided to anyone about the feelings of frustration and restlessness which had been tormenting her for weeks now. In fact it was only this very morning, while she'd been waiting in the queue at the post office, that she'd finally made up her mind to leave Kindarroch and try her luck down south.

'How…how did you know?' she managed faintly.

Morag's eyes twinkled. 'We'll just call it a guess. Anyone can see that a girl like you shouldn't have to waste her time in a backwater like this, just hoping for the best. For the last ten years anyone with an ounce of ambition in them has gone south where the opportunities are.'

Catriona accepted the explanation. 'I suppose you're right. There's no work to be had in Kindarroch, that's for sure.'

'And not much chance of a girl finding a husband either,' Morag added innocently.

Once again Catriona was jolted by surprise, and she quickly covered her embarrassment with a self-conscious laugh. 'I really haven't been giving it that much thought.'

'Haven't you?' Morag asked, regarding her with fond amusement. 'Well, if you say so. But I've an idea there's a rich and handsome young man out there just waiting to fall in love with a girl like you.'

Catriona smiled in embarrassment. 'Away with you. You're just teasing. Anyway, he wouldn't have to be rich…or even that handsome. I'd settle for someone with a kind heart, nice teeth and a sense of humour.'

Morag gave a nod of approval. 'Aye…I know you would. So where are you thinking of going?'

She'd been trying to make her mind up about that. 'I'm not sure. Edinburgh or Glasgow, I suppose. They're not so far away that I can't come back and visit my folks any time I feel homesick.'

Morag shook her head. 'You'll find what you're looking for in London, and you'll be far too busy to feel homesick.'

'London!' Her blue eyes widened doubtfully. That was the south of England! Another planet as far as she was concerned. She was about to reject the idea out of hand when something made her pause. Morag had sounded so sure of herself.

'Why London?' she asked cautiously. 'I don't know a soul down there.'

Morag merely smiled. 'Donald could give you a lift the next time he takes a load of fish to Inverness. There's an overnight train from there that would get you to London the next morning.'

If Morag did know anything she was keeping it to herself, and Catriona still looked doubtful. 'I…I don't know… I've a bit of money saved up but I hear it's a terribly expensive place to live.'

Morag closed her eyes for a moment, as if deep in thought, then she opened them and said with quiet confidence, 'You'll manage. I know you'll have a hard time at first, but I've never met a McNeil yet who's afraid of a challenge. Anyway, you'll meet someone who'll become a good friend. She'll help you to find your feet.'

She didn't much like the sound of the first bit and

she frowned. 'Excuse me, Morag. What exactly do you mean by a "hard time"?'

Morag leaned across the table and patted her hand affectionately. 'I just mean that it's never easy when you suddenly find yourself in a strange place… amongst people you don't know.' She glanced towards the window again, her eyes distant. 'I remember how I felt when I first came here from the islands.'

Catriona wondered if she should be taking this seriously. Shouldn't she just humour and play along with this eccentric but sweet old lady and then be on her way, having done her good deed for the day?

'Aye. I suppose there's something in that, Morag,' she admitted. 'But I'm not expecting a bed of roses.' She finished her tea, then rose and said brightly, 'Perhaps I will go to London. And if I do meet this wonderful man you say is waiting for me I'll be sure to write and let you know.'

An odd little smile played on Morag's lips. 'There will be no need for that, Catriona. I'll know well enough when it happens. Now you'd better go home and break the news to your parents.'

As things turned out she put off telling her parents until after supper that evening. Suddenly the only sound in the room was the heavy ticking of the clock on the mantelpiece as they both stared at her in silence.

She sighed. 'Well, don't look so surprised. You must know it's been on my mind for some time.'

Her parents looked at each other in resignation, then her father nodded. 'Aye, lass. We can't say it's come as a great surprise.' He toyed with his pipe, then cleared his throat. 'Where are you thinking of going?'

'London.'

'London!' exclaimed her mother in horror. 'But that's so far away!' She appealed to her husband, 'Tell her not to go. You're her father. She's only a child!'

'I'm an adult now,' Catriona reminded her gently.

Her mother sniffed. 'Barely. You're still a child as far as I'm concerned.'

'Oh?' She smiled. 'Aren't you forgetting that you were only eighteen when you married Dad? I dare say that Gran said the very same thing about you.'

Her mother sniffed again, but her father chuckled. 'She's got you there, Jean. And a bonnie bride you were.' He grinned at his daughter. 'Don't worry, lass. Your mother doesn't think you're ready for London, but I'm wondering if London is ready for you.'

'I hear it's an awfully wicked place,' her mother warned, 'Gangsters and drugs and terrible tap water you have to filter before you can drink it. Anyway, you were born and raised here. You'll get lost. And all your friends are here.'

'And they're all in the same boat as me,' she replied. 'There's no work here and I've been a burden to you long enough. I can't let you go on supporting me for ever. I've got to stand on my own two feet.' She smiled at both of them, then said quietly, 'Besides, I don't want to end up an old maid. You'll be wanting grandchildren, won't you?'

'Aye…' her mother said wistfully. 'But I'd always hoped that one day you and Jamie Reid would…'

Catriona gave a snort to indicate what she thought of a man who still let his old mother fetch the coal from the back shed.

'She's right,' her father agreed. 'There isn't a lad in Kindarroch I'd want for a son-in-law. All the good ones leave here the first chance they get. They know there's no future in the fishing now. They've all gone south to work in banks or factories.'

Her mother sighed. 'I suppose you're right. I even heard that the Harbour Hotel might soon be up for sale. Trade is that bad.' She looked at Catriona sadly. 'There's no use me trying to make you change your mind. You're just like your father. The McNeils always were a stubborn lot.'

Catriona gave her a kiss on the cheek, then hugged her. 'That's why you married one, isn't it? Maybe I'll be as lucky as you were. Old Morag seems to think so.'

It had been said in all innocence but her mother gave a start and her eyes widened. 'When did you see Morag? Is she the one who's been putting this idea into your head?'

'Och, no,' she answered lightly. 'I helped her home with her shopping this morning and when we got there she invited me in for a cup of tea.'

There was a shocked silence then, 'You were inside her *house*?'

'Aye. And I dare say you'd have done the same if she'd invited you. Anyway, I'd already made up my mind about leaving and I swear on my life I hadn't told anyone. But she knew.'

Her father scratched his head in amused wonder. 'Aye…that's Morag for you. There isn't much goes on around here that she doesn't know about.'

'She has the second sight, right enough,' her mother agreed in a respectful whisper. 'It's no wonder that the poor wee minister takes to drink whenever he sees her.' She paused, then asked with bated breath, 'What's it like inside her house?'

Catriona reassured her. 'Well…it's very old-fashioned but everything is clean and polished. And there wasn't a black cat or crystal ball or black candle in sight, if that's what you're asking.'

'Oh...' It was a sound of disappointment. Then, 'So what exactly did she tell you?'

'She just said that I had nothing to worry about because I was a McNeil and the McNeils had always known how to look after themselves.'

Again her mother sounded disappointed. 'Is that all?'

'Isn't it enough?' she asked, skilfully avoiding a direct answer. 'Haven't you always said that she has the "gift" and that she was a person you could trust?'

'It's good enough for me,' her father said firmly. He bowed to the inevitable with good grace. 'We'll organise a wee going-away party for you in the hotel bar the night before you leave.'

Her mother bit her lip, then nodded and gave a tired smile. 'Aye...I suppose you're right, Catriona. I always knew this day would come. But you'll come back and see us as often as you can, won't you?'

'Of course I will, Mum.' She hugged and kissed them both, then turned away quickly before they could see the tears forming in her eyes.

CHAPTER TWO

WHEN the flat was cleaned and tidied to her personal satisfaction Catriona peeked into Madge's room. Madge was snoring gently, and, careful not to disturb her, Catriona closed the door quietly. Then she put on her coat and locked the flat door as she went out.

The shop was only a ten-minute walk away. Since it was Sunday, a day usually spent lounging around and resting, Catriona was dressed informally in jeans and a loose white cotton sweater. And in spite of the ache in her heart she also wore her usual air of friendliness as she exchanged good mornings with the regulars she was beginning to recognise. Old Nellie who ran the florist shop next door to the boutique was busy setting up her usual brilliant display on the pavement outside and she ordered a bunch of flowers, telling Nellie she'd pick them up when she was finished.

She made herself a cup of coffee, then, arming herself with a stock sheet from the cubby-hole which served as an office, she began checking the inventory in the rear stock room.

The jaunty, carefree smile which she'd worn on the way here had merely been a front. Now that she was alone the mask had slipped, and there was a hard bitterness in her eyes and the downturn of her mouth.

She tried her best, but ten minutes later she felt like giving up. At any other time stock-taking was a chore she could breeze through in half an hour, but this morning she was finding it impossible to concentrate.

Her mind just wasn't on the job. It was too preoccu-
pied with dark feelings of betrayal and seething anger.

How could she have been so stupid as to fall for
that black-hearted devil? So the McNeils could look
after themselves, could they? Well, here was one who
obviously couldn't. Had she surrendered herself to
him so willingly because beneath all her pride she was
nothing more than a gullible Highland peasant girl
who still believed in the folk tales of her race? Tales
about magic and dark lovers and old women who
could foretell the future. Had she wanted to believe
that Ryan Hind was the man she was destined to
marry? Was that the reason she had so carelessly
fallen in love with him? Had she been her own worst
enemy?

The seemingly random hand of fate which had
brought them together had been in the shape of a
young teenage tearaway causing chaos and posing a
threat to life and limb as he'd hurtled along the pavement on a pair of rollerblades.

Catriona had managed to leap out of his way just
in time to save herself from being knocked flat. It had
been more of a sideways stagger, but the end result
had been a collision with the tall stranger who'd just
emerged from the estate agent's office.

'Oops!' she'd gasped, the breath almost knocked
out of her. His arms had held her securely and she'd
stammered an apology to the knot of his silk tie,
which had been all she could see of him at the time.

'I…I'm sorry.'

The deep, warmly resonant voice seemed to wash
over her. 'I'm not. You're welcome. So far this has
been the highlight of my day. You can drop into my
arms any time you want.'

She was about to tell him resentfully that she was quite capable of standing on her own two feet, and that there was no need for him to clasp her so tightly, when she strained her head upwards and changed her mind. Strikingly handsome was the first thought that came to mind. Beneath dark, ironically tilted brows the eyes were a startling light grey, alive and sharply observant. It was a face which instantly evoked visions of romantic encounters under the starlit skies of far-off deserts. It was a face which would cause any woman's heart to flutter nervously.

'Are you hurt?' he asked in concern.

The sound of that voice sent little shivers through her again, and she managed to shake her head. She could smell him in her nostrils. The faint hint of after-shave...the fresh, laundry smell of his blindingly white shirt.

The noise of the rush hour traffic dimmed in her ears and she was oblivious of the people jostling by to catch their buses home. She was alone with him in a pool of silence, struck dumb and absolutely smitten.

His eyes continued to stare down into hers, making her more dry-mouthed than ever. 'With any luck that young thug will break a leg before he causes a serious accident,' he remarked in annoyance.

At last she managed to say breathlessly, 'Yes. It...it isn't safe to walk the streets these days. Some people are so inconsiderate, aren't they?' Now that had been a really brilliant observation, hadn't it? she thought. Why couldn't she have thought of something witty, or at least more interesting to say? But it was hard to be cool and sophisticated when you were feeling hot and flustered. And he still hadn't loosened his grip on her.

'You look a little shaken and pale,' he observed, then added in a voice which brooked no argument, 'What you need is a brandy. Come on.'

Her lips opened in a half-hearted attempt to protest, but nothing came and she allowed herself to be led gently but firmly the few yards along the pavement to the nearest bar. It was not until she found herself being ushered into a seat at a secluded table in the lounge that she managed a nervous stammer. 'I...I don't like brandy. And I really don't think...'

'Whisky, then? I insist you have something.' He eyed her paternally. 'Purely for medicinal purposes only.'

She smiled weakly, overwhelmed by the charm and force of his personality. 'All right, then. A small one. Glenlivet...and some mineral water, please.' That was how the English tourists drank it at the harbour bar, much to the amusement of the locals, so it seemed the sophisticated thing to do.

He summoned a waiter, gave him the order, then sat down facing her. Reaching across the table, he introduced himself. 'I'm Ryan Hind. And you are?'

'Catriona McNeil,' she murmured politely. His hand was firm and cool and sent a tingle up her arm.

He repeated her first name to himself softly, then smiled. 'Very pretty. Suits you admirably.'

She was acutely aware of the way his sharp eyes were assessing her appearance, and the thought passed through her mind that a man like him would never have given her a second glance if he'd met her before Madge had taken her under her wing and given her some tips on style and fashion. It was Madge who supplied the clothes she wore, insisting that it had nothing to do with generosity and everything to do with the image of the shop.

At the moment she was wearing a loose-fitting pearl-grey jacket over a cream silk blouse, and her red hair had been groomed and styled to frame her face and fall in a languid curve to her shoulders.

His eyes continued to study her in a silence which she began to find more embarrassing by the second. Her wits seemed to be deserting her and her left leg had suddenly developed a nervous tremble. God knows what kind of impression she was making on him, she thought desperately. A half-witted schoolgirl could have done better.

'It…it's rather nice in here, isn't it?' she said, making a desperate stab at conversation. 'I pass this place every day but it's the first time I've ever been inside.' Oh, God! If that was the best she could do she might be better keeping her mouth shut.

One dark eyebrow rose in obvious interest. 'You live here in Chelsea, do you?'

'Yes. Palmerston Court. It's only a few minutes' walk from here.'

He nodded. 'I know it. A very exclusive and desirable property. I've been thinking of buying a flat there myself. I'm needing some place permanent. And you would definitely recommend it—as an investment, say?'

She was beginning to recover her scrambled wits. Could it really be possible that this gorgeous man was actually interested in her? It seemed unbelievable, and yet… She reviewed the past few minutes since they'd met. One moment she'd been strolling home, minding her own business, and the next she'd been thrust inelegantly into his arms. It had been a highly unlikely

start to a meaningful relationship, yet stranger things
had happened. He could simply have smiled politely,
released her and let her go without another word. But
he hadn't. He'd held her tightly, expressed concern,
brought her here for a drink, asked her her name, paid
her a compliment and found out where she lived. Now
he was asking her advice! Oh, there was no doubt
about it. This was Mr Right and no mistake. If this
wasn't love then why did she feel six inches off the
ground?

He was still waiting for her answer and she gave a
tentative self-conscious smile. 'I don't know much
about property. You'd be better asking an expert.'

The suggestion brought a cynical smile to his lips.
'There's no such thing as an "expert" in the property
business these days. I've always found that it pays to
get your information from the people on the ground,
as it were. Perhaps you'd be kind enough to show me
over the place some time? Do you have a flatmate
or…parents you'd have to ask?'

'My parents live in Scotland,' she said quickly,
then added a little defensively, 'I'm old enough to
look after myself.'

He seemed amused. 'I'm sure you are, Catriona. I
admire a spirit of independence. So you live in
London all by yourself, do you?'

At the moment, while Madge was on holiday, she
did, and some devil within, urging her to project an
image of maturity and self-reliance, made her keep
silent about Madge. Thankfully she was spared the
necessity of an outright spoken lie by the arrival of
the waiter with their order.

Forestalling any further questions on that subject,

she busied herself by daintily topping up her whisky from the bottle of mineral water.

The grey eyes watched her with amused interest, then he said with approval, 'I'm impressed and pleased to see that you didn't order some ghastly cocktail garnished with a paper umbrella. A nice malt whisky instead. You're obviously a lady of discernment.'

The compliment gave her a warm glow. He said the nicest things…and with such sincerity. She was a lady. A lady of discernment, no less! And he had such lovely white teeth when he smiled. Oh, it was too much. He was bound to have a girlfriend somewhere. Quickly pushing that unwelcome thought aside, she raised her glass and sipped far more than she'd intended. Immediately she felt it go to her head. At least the water had quenched the fire of the spirit and she was mercifully spared the embarrassment of having a coughing fit.

'Do you have many friends in Chelsea?' he asked casually. 'An attractive girl like you surely has a boyfriend or two.'

'Oh, no,' she assured him quickly. Perhaps too quickly. She paused and assumed an air of nonchalance. 'At least nothing to write home about.'

'So there's no one special in your life?'

She shrugged. 'Not really.' Her heart was hammering away inside her chest.

'London can be a very lonely place,' he commented quietly. 'You must have some kind of social life, surely?'

She didn't want him getting the idea that she was some kind of stick-in-the-mud, a stay-at-home, so she said blithely, 'Well, there's the usual round of parties.

You know what Chelsea is like. There's always something going on.'

He grinned and seemed satisfied. Suddenly he glanced at the expensive gold watch on his wrist and she felt the stab of cold disappointment. He was going to finish his drink, make some excuse, then be on his way—and she'd never see him again. Was it because of something she'd said? Had he seen through her lies...even if they had just been little white ones?

What did a woman do at a moment like this? she asked herself desperately. Simply shrug off her disappointment? Console herself with the thought that he wasn't meant to be the one, after all? Perhaps fate had someone else in mind for her, and that was a pity because she was quite willing to settle for him here and now. Given such a short acquaintance it might be foolish to imagine that she was hopelessly already in love, but how else could she explain this wild beating of her heart?

He still had that oddly penetrating and quizzical look in his eye when he asked suddenly, 'Are you sure you've quite recovered, Catriona?'

She managed a bright smile. 'Yes. I'm fine, thanks.'

'Well, I'm glad to hear it.' He gave a sigh of regret. 'I'd love to sit here and chat all day and get to know you better, but I'm afraid I have to leave. I'm meeting a client back at my hotel in fifteen minutes.'

She knew it had been too good to be true. Somehow she contrived another cheerful smile. 'Please don't let me keep you from your work. You've been very kind and I appreciate it, Mr Hind.'

'Good. Then perhaps you'd like to show that appreciation by having dinner with me this evening?'

She replaced her glass on the table, stared at it stupidly for a moment, then looked up to see if he was serious.

'Th—this evening?' she stammered.

'In two hours' time, to be exact,' he said pleasantly. 'But if that's too short a notice for you I can arrange it for later.'

'No!' she said quickly. 'I mean…I'm sure I can manage that.'

'Good,' he said briskly. Then with a devastating smile he added, 'It's been one of those days. Dinner with you will make up for everything.'

Her mind was racing ahead. What would she wear? Did she have anything remotely suitable for a dinner date?

'I'll leave the choice to you, Catriona,' he said gallantly. 'I usually dine at Cardini's but perhaps you'd prefer French…or Italian?'

'Cardini's will do fine, Mr Hind,' she answered lightly. She had no idea what Cardini's was like, but if a man with his grooming and style ate there regularly it was sure to be first rate. He'd probably be wearing a dinner jacket and bow tie, and God knows what *she* was going to wear but she'd think of something.

He flashed another smile. 'Enough of the Mr Hind. Call me Ryan.'

She hoped she didn't look as flushed as she felt when she smiled back. 'Very well…Ryan.' Seeing him glance at his watch again, she hurriedly finished her drink then said, 'I, too, will have to be going.'

His hand claimed her arm lightly as he escorted her outside. At the doorway he paused. 'I'll send a car to pick you up at seven-thirty. Will that be all right, Catriona?'

'Yes…' Her voice had gone husky with excitement. 'I…I'll tell the security man in the foyer to look out for it.'

He smiled again, then turned, and she watched him stride off. For a moment she simply stood there, hardly daring to believe what had happened. Something was bound to go wrong. He'd change his mind. She'd get all dressed up and sit waiting for a car which would never show up.

But then again perhaps he really *did* mean it, and he would send a car, and she'd damn well better be ready just in case. But what was she going to wear?

With a sudden flash of inspiration she hurried back to the shop and let herself in. Telling herself that Madge would understand, she made straight for the reject corner in the stock room.

She found the dress she wanted and held it at arm's length, then swallowed nervously. Would she dare wear this? Strapless, in pale green Chinese silk, it carried a top designer name and a price tag that would have bought a good second-hand car.

To the casual observer it was a sublime creation and worth every penny, but to eagle-eyed Madge who'd spotted the tiny imperfection in the hemline, it was worthless. As in all such cases she'd immediately got in touch with her supplier, who invariably told Madge to get rid of the items in any way she saw fit. Madge usually donated them to the charity shops in the East End. It tickled her sense of humour to think of some poor old cleaning lady going to work in a five-hundred-pound coat she'd bought for next to nothing.

Catriona found a matching silk stole, then she wrapped them up, let herself out of the shop and rushed back to the flat.

The internal phone buzzed at seven-thirty precisely. She answered it breathlessly, then rushed over to the window and saw the long black limousine drawn up in the forecourt below. Then, breathing deeply to calm herself, she took one last look at herself in the mirror.

When she'd first tried on the dress she'd eyed her reflection in despair. She'd never have the nerve to go out in this! She couldn't wear a bra—not that that was a problem with the way it clung to her figure— but the amount of flesh and cleavage on display could only be justified in front of a husband or doctor. But it certainly looked stunning. She'd turned this way and that, getting used to the idea.

Now she completed the outfit with the stole and one of Madge's coats, borrowed for the occasion, then took the lift down to the foyer where Charlie, the security man, had to look twice before grinning and wishing her a pleasant evening.

In the back of the chauffeur-driven car she glanced at herself in the vanity mirror. Although she wore no make-up except for a touch of lipstick, her colour was high. It was nerves, she told herself. High as a kite. She'd have to relax.

She'd have to try and be smart and sophisticated, like the women who came into the shop. They drawled their words and called everyone 'dahling' and…well, perhaps she needn't go that far…they had what she supposed was style.

Could she carry it off or was she going to blow it? Was she just going to sit throughout the evening overawed and tongue-tied until he got bored to death with her company?

She scowled at her reflection, then felt gooseflesh on her neck as she imagined she heard the voice of Morag whispering in her ear— 'I've never met a McNeil yet who's afraid of a challenge.' She blinked and drew a deep breath. Voices in her head? That was all she needed! Still, Morag had been right. This was a challenge, and win or lose she was going to give it her best shot.

The traffic in the West End was in its usual state of chaos, but soon enough the limousine drew up outside the restaurant. The chauffeur opened the rear door for her and as she stepped on to the pavement the restaurant doorman came over and tipped his hat. 'Miss McNeil?'

'Yes?'

'Mr Hind is expecting you.'

He led her into the foyer, where a cloakroom attendant took charge of her coat and stole, then on into the restaurant proper, where the dignified head waiter took charge and escorted her through the length of the room towards a table in a quiet, exclusive corner.

Her stomach began to flutter nervously as she took in her surroundings. The hushed, refined dignity of the place was almost intimidating. Silver, gleaming under candlelight...the subdued murmur of conversation...the discreet clink of bottles against wine glasses...the plush Victorian decor...

Suddenly there he was, resplendent in dinner jacket, just as she'd imagined. He rose to his feet with a welcoming smile. 'Catriona.' He looked her over with approval. 'You look stunning in that dress!'

'Thank you,' she murmured, glowing inwardly at

the compliment. Encouraged by his reaction, she smiled as she sat down. 'I'm glad you like it. It was a problem making up my mind what to wear. I only decided on this at the last moment.' Oh, you wicked little liar! she thought. She could hardly believe she'd said that.

The waiter handed her a menu but she brushed it aside. 'I'll leave the choice to you, Ryan. What would you recommend?'

His mouth twitched in humorous acknowledgement of her faith in his judgement and he said promptly, 'Duck in orange sauce. It's the chef's speciality.' When the waiter had gone with the order he continued, 'I took the liberty of ordering a decent wine before you arrived. If it's too dry for your liking I'll have them bring something else.'

She wouldn't have cared if it was cold bathwater, she thought as she watched him pour a glass. Raising it to her mouth, she took a delicate sip, savoured it for a moment, then nodded and dabbed daintily at her lips with her napkin. 'Very nice,' she murmured. 'Just the way I like it.' Would you just listen to her? She, who wouldn't know the difference between claret and cooking sherry!

She took comfort from the fact that she wasn't really deceiving him. It was just that since she'd accepted his invitation she was obligated to see that she didn't spoil his evening. She had to make an effort to make herself sound agreeable and interesting. And it was working! She could tell by the way those eyes of his seldom left her face.

There was one sticky moment, when he asked her whereabouts in Scotland her parents lived.

'Oh, you'll never have heard of it,' she said casually. 'It's called Kindarroch. In the Western Highlands. Nothing much goes on up there.'

'And that's why you decided to come and live in London?' he suggested with an understanding smile. 'You certainly don't look like one of the hunting, shooting and fishing set. I somehow can't see you tramping over the estate in gumboots with the Labrador at your heels.'

Estate, she thought? Who'd mentioned anything about an estate? Still, if he wanted to believe that she was one of the minor Scottish aristocracy that was fine by her. When they got to know each other better they'd laugh about it together. But it only went to prove that she seemed to have 'style' after all.

He had lovely hands, she thought as she watched him refill her glass. Well-formed and well-manicured, sensitive, yet strong and competent-looking. He had a thick gold ring set with a ruby on his little finger.

There was something else she was beginning to notice about him, and that was the aura of power and unspoken authority evident in the relaxed way he conducted himself. His mere presence seemed to dominate the room. The hovering waiters were always ready with a fresh bottle or a clean napkin at his slightest gesture. And she doubted if there was a woman in the place who didn't keep glancing towards him.

Looking back on it now, she still wasn't clear how she'd ended up back in his hotel suite. It was true that the wine had gone to her head, but she remembered agreeing enthusiastically with him when he'd said that the night was still young and that it would be a pity to end their new-found friendship when the meal was over. It had been words to that effect, anyway, but the undeniable fact was that she had been out of her depth and completely under his spell. She'd been captivated...enthralled...enraptured... And the thought of the consequences had never entered her head.

It had only been when they were in his spacious, luxurious lounge, and he'd removed his jacket and tie and invited her to kick off her shoes and make herself comfortable, that she'd had the first stirrings of doubt about the situation she'd landed herself in.

Well, it was too late now, wasn't it? she'd thought. And, anyway, the man was a gentleman—anyone could see that. If he became over-amorous she would make it quite clear to him that she wasn't that kind of girl and he wouldn't push the matter. He'd probably respect her all the more, wouldn't he?

As he'd poured a couple of drinks at the built-in bar he'd pressed a remote control. The lights had dimmed and soft music came from hidden speakers. Looking around, she hadn't failed to be impressed by the size and sheer luxury of the place.

'Do you always stay in hotels like this?' she asked with a frown. 'It must be terribly expensive. Wouldn't it be cheaper to have a flat of your own?'

'Cheaper, yes,' he agreed. 'But not nearly so convenient.' He handed her a glass, then raised his hand to stroke and feel the soft texture of her hair. 'A man only needs a house if he feels the desire to put down roots, Catriona. But that only happens if he's lucky enough to find a very special woman. Some woman to share his life and his dreams of raising a family.'

The backs of his fingers were lightly brushing the soft, tender skin of her neck and the glass trembled in her hand. 'I...I'm sure you will, Ryan,' she said with the breath catching in her throat. She suddenly needed to sit down…badly…but his eyes were holding her with an enervating magnetism.

'Yes…' he breathed softly. 'Perhaps I already have, Catriona. I was giving up hope until now.'

'W-were you?'

'Why do you think I asked you about the flats in Palmerston Court?'

She gulped. 'As…as an investment, you said…'

He smiled at her innocence. 'Let's just say that the instant fate thrust you into my arms I knew my dreams hadn't been in vain.' He gently removed the drink from her shaking hand and placed it beside his own on the coffee table, then he took her by the shoulders and looked down into the depths of her wide blue eyes.

Her mind was a chaotic mess of emotions. Was he truly telling her that she was that 'special' woman? Well, why not? Love at first sight was a fact of life, wasn't it? It might be the stuff of romantic dreams and fairy tales but it did happen. It had happened to her, so why shouldn't it happen to him? Those impossibly clear and luminous grey eyes were filling her vision now, and all sense of critical judgement was swamped by her desire to believe him.

His voice was suddenly low and husky with desire. 'You're a very beautiful woman, Catriona. I've never seen lips that look so kissable and tempting as yours. They have the power to drive a man into mad impulsiveness.'

His arms pulled her closer until she was crushed against him, so hard she could feel the strong, steady and relentless beat in his chest, then her own heart skipped and began to race as his mouth slowly descended on hers. The contact of warm, sweet and yielding flesh drove every thought from her mind and she abandoned herself to the thrill of his sensual provocation. A low moan bubbled in her throat as his tongue parted her lips, exposing her to a hitherto unknown and unguessed at height of passion.

The kiss left her dazed and breathless, and she rested her head against his shoulder, seeking time to recover. He kept holding her in the imprisoning embrace of his arms, then he began nuzzling at her ear with his lips.

In a hoarse whisper he said, 'I'd be less than a man if I didn't confess and tell you that there is nothing in this world I want more than to make love to you, darling. No woman has ever made me feel this way before. You have a beauty I can't resist. I want to make wonderful love to you, Catriona. I want to give you all I have to offer. We can give each other so much pleasure and happiness. I want to possess you and never, ever let you go.'

She closed her eyes tightly and bit down on her already swollen lip. How could she reject that passionate plea from the heart or ignore the promise in his words? Could she allow her old-fashioned conscience to stand in the way of an honestly declared love?

The choice was simple. She could tearfully refuse, grab her coat and scamper to safety like a timid rabbit, or she could be mature about this and do what every throbbing and aching nerve in her body was demanding.

She felt the slight tug as he undid the zip at her back, and as the silk dress slid down over her slim body to fall in a whisper at her feet she turned her face upwards, seeking his lips once again, certain in the belief that all this had been written in the stars.

CHAPTER THREE

MADGE called into the shop and dragged Catriona off to lunch, leaving the part-time assistant to hold the fort for a couple of hours.

The food at the Wheatsheaf was always excellent, but the meal was in danger of being spoiled, for Catriona at least, by the snatches of loud conversation drifting from the two women at the next table.

'...sent the damned thing back to him, dahling. I mean...he knew I wanted a Jeep as a run-about. Everyone has a four-wheel drive these days...'

'...a nice figure, I grant you. But who the hell is she? I heard that her father is a pig farmer down in Essex!'

'...bald and hopeless in bed, but he has this marvellous luxury cruiser in the Med. So naturally I...'

They made Catriona squirm. If you stayed in this part of London long enough you began to recognise the type. Usually in their early twenties, they were full of shallow pretensions and mannerisms and their empty lives revolved around social position, money and sex—in that order.

When they finally got up and left she looked across the table at Madge and said in exasperation, 'Did you hear them? What an exhibition of conceit and arrogance and sheer...'

'Yes, dear,' Madge said mildly. 'I think everyone heard them, and now they're hearing you.'

'Hmph! I don't care. I feel better getting it off my

chest.' The chicken in honey and ginger sauce tasted better now, and she savoured a piece before commenting bitterly, 'You won't believe this, Madge, but I tried to model myself on women like them when I went out with Ryan Hind. I thought it was the way to attract men. I was trying to be smart and sophisticated.'

'Well, you certainly attracted him, didn't you?' She fixed Catriona with a stern, reproving eye, then relented. 'I'm sorry. That was a crass thing to say. But it's been over a month now since you found out the truth. You should be over it by now.'

Catriona sighed and stared at her plate gloomily. 'I've tried to forget it…put it down to experience as you suggested…but I can't. I…I lie in bed at night and he's there in the darkness, whispering his lies in my ear. When I close my eyes I see his face and his treacherous smile. And when I do manage to get to sleep he's still there, haunting my dreams.'

Madge looked at her dryly. 'That sounds to me like you're still in love with the rogue.'

She looked up, startled. 'In love with *him*!' Her voice cracked in protest. 'After the way he treated me!'

'Oh, you'd be surprised at the folly of some women,' Madge proclaimed, helping herself to a large sip of vodka and tomato juice. 'They just can't resist playing with fire. The worse a man's reputation the stronger the attraction. They delude themselves into believing that all it needs to make him change his ways is the love of a really good woman.'

Catriona lowered her eyes, then viciously stabbed at another morsel of chicken, wishing it was Ryan Hind's heart. Still in love with him! That was rich!

'Look…' she said, after a moment. 'You invited me here to lunch, and I'm sure it wasn't just to sit and listen to me moaning about my troubles.'

'You're wrong,' Madge announced with a smile. 'That's exactly why I brought you here. But before we go into that…' She delved into her handbag and laid a small gift-wrapped box on the table. 'That's for you, my dear. A small token of my appreciation.'

Catriona gave her a puzzled look, then with curiosity began to undo the wrapping.

'I dropped in to see my accountant this morning,' Madge informed her. 'He tells me that the takings in the shop have gone up twenty per cent since you began working for me.'

'Oh? Well, that's good news, but I'm sure I can't take all the credit,' Catriona said modestly. 'It's more likely to be that new range of Italian skirt-suits we're stocking. They're selling like hot cakes.'

Madge dismissed her protest with a wave of a well-manicured hand. 'Credit where it's due. The customers really like you, my dear. I've watched you in action. You're not pushy and you're always pleasant. More importantly, though, you've got a natural instinct for good taste. If a customer chooses something that doesn't suit them you tell them straight to their face.' She gave a throaty chuckle. 'Oh, I know some of them get the hump and march out with their noses in the air—you see, they aren't used to shop girls doing that sort of thing—but they come back a few days later, and the word spreads that they've finally found a shop which puts its reputation before sales figures.'

'Well…if you say so.' Catriona murmured, secretly pleased. The wrapping was off now and she opened

he lid. Her eyes widened and she gasped as she removed the gleaming gold bracelet from its bed of
black velvet.

'It's beautiful!' She looked at Madge self-
consciously. 'It…it must have been awfully expensive. You shouldn't be giving me presents like this!
It's embarrassing.'

'Don't tell me what to do with my money, young
lady,' Madge admonished her with a fond smile. 'That
little bauble is meant to cheer you up and get you
back on form. You haven't been your usual bright-
eyed self lately, have you?'

She accepted the rebuke with a weak smile of apology. 'I…I suppose not.'

'You're damn right you haven't. And the reason is
obvious, isn't it?' Madge paused, eyed her thoughtfully for a moment, then asserted dryly, 'That really
must have been a night to remember if it's still got
you glassy-eyed after all this time.' She leaned across
the table and lowered her voice. 'So tell me…woman
to woman…are all the things I've been hearing about
him true?'

'What things?' Catriona asked warily.

'Is he as good in bed as they say he is?'

A question like that would have shocked her a
month ago, which only went to show how sheltered
and innocent her life had been in Kindarroch. But this
was London and this was Madge, and between them
both she was rapidly getting an education.

'Can't we discuss this tonight back at the flat?' she
asked in a frantic whisper.

'No. I'm going away for a couple of days. I'm
catching the evening flight to Paris. An old flame of

mine has invited me over for a house-warming. He'
just bought a château.'

Catriona smiled to herself. Madge seemed to have
enough old flames to set fire to a rain-soaked forest
'That sounds exciting,' she said. 'I hope you have a
nice time.'

'I will.' Madge assured her. 'He's a sweet old thing
Now answer my question. Satisfy my curiosity. How
would you rate Ryan Hind as a lover?'

'I've no idea,' she answered stiffly. 'He was the
first and quite possibly the last lover I've ever had, so
I've no one else to compare him to, have I?'

Madge gave a delicate cough. 'Pardon me. I was
forgetting. Well, let's put it another way. Did he make
the earth move, as they say in novels? You don't have
to go into the details. A general impression will do.'

There was no way of getting out of this. Madge
could be like a terrier after a rabbit when she wanted
to. Catriona almost blushed, but managed to remain
calm in spite of the memories and passionate emotions the question evoked.

Her strongest emotion was one of guilt at the willingness with which she'd surrendered. But there was
also the undeniable fact that her own awakened sexual
desire and the apparent loving tenderness he'd used
to inflame that desire had been a combination impossible to resist.

His touch had been electrifying, and as his hands
had explored and moulded and caressed every contour
of her body she'd closed her eyes and let herself
drown in a warm sea of sensual delight and rapture.
She'd felt the vigorous hardening of his own yearning
as he'd crushed her to him, then she'd clung to him

in a fever as he'd lifted and cradled her in his arms and carried her to his bedroom.

His loving had been slow and exquisitely controlled, turning every nerve into incandescent flame until at last he'd thrust deeper and faster and brought her to a heart-stopping, dizzying climax. She'd gasped and moaned and raked her fingers down his back, only half hearing his own groan of satisfied release.

Suddenly she was brought back to earth by the sound of Madge's amused voice, 'All right! That dreamy look on your face says it all. Then I can take it that the stories about his prowess are all true?'

Catriona cleared her throat and said primly, 'I was the only one wearing L-plates that night. He certainly seemed to know what he was doing.'

Madge raised her eyebrows. 'Well, I should bloody well think so, considering the amount of practice he gets!'

Catriona toyed with her fork and wished that Madge would change the subject but Madge didn't.

'What puzzles me,' she went on, 'is why you were so surprised when you saw his picture in the paper and discovered that he was going with someone else. Surely you must have had your suspicions about him when you awoke in the morning and found your taxi fare on the table? I mean...how much of a hint does a girl need?'

She bit her lip, looked at Madge helplessly, then shook her head, more in wonder at her own innocence than anything else. 'No...I didn't. He'd already told me that he was a busy businessman and I thought that since I'd still been asleep he'd left me undisturbed out of consideration. And, anyway, there was that note promising to get in touch with me as soon as he got back.' She gave a laugh of self-mockery. 'That shows the kind of fool I was, doesn't it?'

Madge regarded her with sorrow. 'Your misfortune was to fall in love with him. Any other girl would have realised that he'd only been looking for a one-night stand, but you're so guileless and innocent. I don't like saying this, dear, but you're going to make an even bigger fool of yourself if you keep on brooding about it like this. You have your whole adult life ahead of you. All men aren't like Ryan Hind. Some day you'll meet someone decent, who really loves you, and you'll get married and raise a lovely family.'

'And how can I tell if a man is decent or a…a rat like him?' she demanded hotly. 'I was wrong once and I could be wrong the next time, couldn't I?' Her face hardened. 'Well, there won't be a next time. I'll make damn sure of that.'

Madge sighed in frustration. 'It's just as I feared.' She pressed her lips together, then said, 'You, young lady, are in danger of turning into a disillusioned and sour old maid. We'll have to do something about that before it's too late, won't we?'

Catriona stared at Madge in silence, her blue eyes perplexed. This was her own personal problem…a problem of her own making, caused by her own stupidity. Madge's sympathy was understandable, but she was acting as if she was the one who'd been betrayed.

'You are suffering from a personality crisis,' Madge went on relentlessly. 'You're beginning to lose your sparkle and your youthful exuberance, and that's bad for business.'

Bad for business? She gave Madge a long, perceptive look, then smiled wryly. 'You're a terrible liar, Madge. That isn't the reason at all, is it?'

Madge returned the smile, then shrugged. 'I know, but the truth is too embarrassing to admit.'

'Huh! I doubt if you've ever been embarrassed in your life.'

'No. I don't suppose I have,' Madge admitted cheerfully. 'But then I've always been a selfish bitch. The only person I ever really cared about was myself. But they say that every woman has a mother instinct. Well, mine has been about twenty years late in arriving, so let's just say that I'm trying belatedly to make amends.' She paused, and for a moment her eyes were filled with a sadness that suddenly made her seem vulnerable, then she brightened up. 'Just look on me as a shop-soiled old fairy godmother who hates to see you unhappy.'

Catriona felt a little humbled by Madge's confession and her eyes misted. 'You have a beautiful soul, Madge, and you're the best friend a girl could have, but I don't want you to get involved in this. I'll deal with it in my own way.'

'Ah, yes…by getting your revenge on him. That's what you said, wasn't it? Something about being the hand of vengeance.' She took another sip of her drink, then shuddered. 'I've been having visions of a tribe of hairy Scotsmen marching over the border, waving their sporrans and broadswords. I hope it won't come to that.'

'Take my word for it, it won't,' Catriona assured her. No one back home would ever hear of this if she had anything to do with it. When she did return to Kindarroch she would be able to do so with her head held high.

'I've never been a great believer in revenge my-self,' Madge said thoughtfully. 'Life's too short to waste time and energy on such a negative ambition. In my experience people like Ryan Hind usually get their comeuppance without any help from their vic-tims. But I'd say that in your case there might be some merit in the idea. It's the only way you're going to get him out of your system and regain your self-respect. So the sooner you get it over and done with the better.'

Madge was right, she thought bitterly. It really was a case of standing up for herself and letting that man know that he had no right to use her then discard her like a piece of trash.

'I've been thinking of little else,' she admitted tiredly. 'But I just don't know how to go about it. My mind keeps going round in circles, getting nowhere. I'd gladly drop a ton of garbage from a very great height if I could only be sure that he'd be directly underneath.'

'Precisely the point I want to make,' said Madge. 'The first thing in any campaign is to know your en-emy, as the old major was fond of telling me. You have to know their weaknesses and know the best way to exploit them.'

Catriona shook her head in frustration. 'I know next to nothing about him, Madge. I can't even remember the name of the hotel he took me to.'

Madge raised a hand in benediction. 'Bless you, my child. It's lucky for you that I'm here to help. It so happens that I've been making it my business during the last few weeks to find out as much as I can about our friend Mr Hind.'

She blinked in surprise. 'You never said anything to me.'

'I was hoping that it wouldn't be necessary, dear.' She took another fortifying drink from her glass then began. 'Ryan Hind is thirty-two years old. An extremely successful property developer. He specialises in the entertainment and leisure industry and he seems to have the knack of knowing which areas are ripe for investment. Either that or he has spies in local government.'

'I'd go for the second option,' Catriona muttered.

'He's never been married,' Madge went on. 'Never even had a steady girlfriend as far as anyone knows. He's a bit of a mystery, really. He was born to wealthy parents on an estate in Surrey, spent four years at Cambridge University, then was offered a commission in the Army. One of those cloak-and-dagger regiments that don't officially exist. He won a couple of medals then resigned his commission four years ago and went into business.'

Catriona snorted. 'He was caught in bed with the CO's wife. I suppose.'

'No. They say that it was because he refused to carry out certain orders he was given.'

'Well, that's not surprising. I can't imagine him taking orders from anyone.' She scowled at the thought. 'I'll bet he was an only child. He can't have a sister, that's for sure, or he'd treat women with more respect.'

Madge nodded in agreement. 'He did, however, have a younger stepbrother. When his father died his mother had remarried. The stepbrother was Malcolm Grant. I say ''was'' because he was killed two years ago in a car crash. Ironic, really, because they say he

was a very promising young racing-driver who could
have been the next world champion. Ryan took the
death very hard.'

Catriona bit her lip. She didn't want to hear things
like that. She'd simply have to steel herself against
any natural feelings of sympathy. Anyway, none of
that had anything to do with the callous way he'd
gone about seducing and then abandoning her. She
didn't see that this was getting her anywhere and she
said so to Madge.

'Background, my dear,' Madge said patiently. 'One
never knows what tiny, seemingly irrelevant nugget
of information might come in useful.'

She conceded the point with a sigh. 'Yes…I dare
say you're right.' She took a sip of her mineral water
and tried to recall anything he'd said to her that might
reveal some weak spot in his armour, but it was a
waste of time. People like Ryan Hind would make
sure they had no weak spots. Not even a conscience
to trouble them. They were the icy cold predators in
the sea of life.

She wondered what she'd do if he were to walk
through that door right now with his latest girlfriend
clinging to his arm. She closed her eyes, slipped the
lead from her imagination and let it roam free like a
slow motion film, the scenario unfolded in her mind…

He would pause in the doorway and the murmur of
conversation would die away, his mere appearance
enough to charge the atmosphere. Women would
breath a little more rapidly at the powerful, charis-
matic image he projected and their partners would
regard him with hostility. His grey eyes would dis-
passionately survey the room until they alighted on
her and then…incredibly…he would smile! Her heart

would begin thudding in her ears as he approached her table. She knew it! It had all been a terrible mistake! He'd simply forgotten where she lived. He'd been frantically searching for weeks and now he'd found her! He'd be only a couple of yards from her and then she would freeze as she saw the smile for what it really was—a cold and distant acknowledgement that he'd once met her briefly. Stricken, she'd watch him pass by without a word. He and his companion would settle themselves at the next table and she would watch as he leaned over and whispered in the girl's ear. The girl would glance across at her, then smirk, whispering something back to him, and they'd both begin laughing. Enraged, she'd get to her feet, march over, snatch the carafe of water from the table and empty it over his head...

'Excuse me...' a voice cut in. 'Have you fallen asleep?'

She jerked her eyes open and smiled awkwardly at Madge. 'Sorry...I was daydreaming.'

'Hmm... We were discussing Ryan Hind, remember?'

'How could I forget? The more I think about him the angrier I get. If there was just some way I could get my hands around his neck.' She almost ground her teeth and narrowed her eyes. 'Sometimes I wish I was a man.'

'Don't we all, my dear? But, since we're women, it has to be a case of superior intelligence versus superior brawn. So it is written in the book of life. So let's apply ourselves to the problem without indulging in any flights of fancy.'

Catriona gave a nod of resignation. The talk of superior intelligence depressed her. She was beginning to think that she'd left her brain back in Kindarroch. Then a sudden thought made her catch her breath, and she glanced to either side before whispering excitedly, 'We know one thing for certain. We know that he dines at Cardini's every night. What if I was to go in there one evening…go straight to his table and…and empty a jug of water over his head?'

Madge didn't look too impressed. 'Too tame,' she remarked. Then she looked thoughtful. 'It does have possibilities, however. You really want to humiliate the wretch, don't you?'

'Damned right I do. And in front of as many people as possible.' Her eyes brightened at the prospect. 'What better place than in the middle of a crowded restaurant? Not just any restaurant, mind you. Cardini's, where all the top people go.'

A mischievous smile played over Madge's lips. 'Cardini's is fine, but I think you can play to an even bigger audience, my dear. The London papers would love to have a picture of Ryan Hind receiving his just deserts at the hands of a scorned woman. It would be worth half a million extra copies at least.'

Catriona eyes widened. 'But…but how?'

'Oh, I could easily arrange that,' Madge said airily. 'A dear old friend of mine who runs a news agency owes me a few favours. He'd have one of his photographers there to record the scene for posterity.' She chuckled at the thought, then added, 'It would have to be something a bit more original than emptying water over him, though. Something that would have the whole town talking.'

Was there anyone in London Madge didn't know? she wondered. 'Well, I can't think of anything else,' she admitted.

Madge remained thoughtful, then she smiled. 'I knew a woman who once had occasion to humiliate a man in public. He was a respected Member of Parliament but by the time she was finished with him he had to resign his seat.' She chuckled and shook her head. 'I doubt if you could bring yourself to go to such lengths, though.'

'Why?' Catriona demanded indignantly. 'The McNeils are slow to anger, but once our minds are made up we're never squeamish about the means of redressing an insult.'

'Hmmm…' Madge said, eyeing her thoughtfully. 'You might have to leave London for a couple of weeks afterwards. Just until the dust has settled. Then I'll let you know when it's safe to return.'

She looked at the older woman cautiously. 'It's nothing illegal, is it? I won't have any part in…'

'Not really illegal…but it would require a considerable amount of acting skill.'

She relaxed and said eagerly, 'In the school play I was Ophelia in *Hamlet*.'

Madge's mouth twitched in amusement. 'The part you'll have to play is that of a woman with more fire in her belly than the fair Ophelia ever had.'

She frowned, then shrugged. 'I can still do it.'

Madge studied her a moment longer, then said with finality, 'We'll see. Now we'll leave it for the moment, my dear. We'll discuss it further in a couple of days, when I get back from France.' She raised her glass and smiled. 'Here's to the sinking of the Golden Hind.'

CHAPTER FOUR

CATRIONA shivered in the chilly evening air. It was draughty and uncomfortable standing in this shop doorway, and although this outfit she was wearing might be all the rage on the catwalks of Paris it had obviously been designed with titillation rather than protection from the elements in mind.

When Madge had returned from France and got round to explaining the scheme she had in mind Catriona had listened with growing apprehension, and when she'd seen the outfit she was expected to wear she'd almost rebelled on the spot. The bright red stiletto-heeled shoes she could put up with, and the matching leather shoulder bag looked OK. But the white spiral-laced trousers and crop top which would leave her with a wide expanse of bare midriff gave her the shudders. And to top it all there was the most outrageous pink-tinted platinum blonde wig she'd ever seen.

She'd looked askance at Madge and protested, 'This is ridiculous! If I don't catch my death of cold I'll get arrested for indecency!'

'No, you won't. The West End is full of girls dressed far more provocatively. Anyway, the more indecent you look the better. When you waltz into Cardini's we want the diners to be in no doubt as to what you do for a living. Now stop complaining and try them on.'

She had done so, reluctantly, and the sight that had

greeted her in the mirror had made her wince. 'My God! I've gone to bed wearing more than this! You can see through the damn thing! I might as well be naked!'

'The most anyone can see is your underwear, and you wouldn't think twice about wearing a skimpy bikini on a beach, would you?' Madge had pointed out calmly.

'That isn't the same, and you know it.'

Madge had ignored the remark, run a critical eye over her then given a satisfied nod. 'It's perfect. Of course, on the night you go there you'll be smothered in make-up. Lots of mascara and bright red lip-gloss. With that and the wig your own mother wouldn't recognise you.'

Thank God for that, she'd thought fervently! Then the obvious conclusion had dawned on her and she'd looked at Madge in dismay. 'That means that Ryan Hind might not recognise me either!'

'You'd better hope he doesn't.'

'But why?' she'd asked with a disappointed frown. 'I want him to know it's me. Hiding behind another identity seems…seems cowardly.'

'Yes… Well, discretion is the better part of valour, as they say. Believe me, my dear, it'll be safer this way. Ryan Hind is going to be one very angry man.' She'd put her forefinger to her chin, tilted her head to one side and smiled. 'We'll call you Trixie Trotter. How does that sound?'

'Abominable.'

'Good. Now…it'll take a few days to get everything organised, so until then you can keep practising your Cockney street-girl accent.'

Well, everything was now in place. Somehow

Madge had found out that Ryan would be dining that night with a companion, and the photographer was already inside, occupying a nearby strategic table.

She'd chosen this doorway because it was directly opposite the imposing entrance to Cardini's and provided a good view of the taxis disembarking their passengers. Her stomach fluttered with nerves. How she'd ever talked herself into this was a mystery. Had it been a desire to impress Madge with her determination or just a wish to prove to herself that she had all the courage and resource of a McNeil?

The worst part of it was having to ignore the stares of the passers-by. Although she'd only been here about ten minutes she'd already been approached by two prospective 'clients'. With the first one it had taken her a moment or two to realise what he was suggesting, and she'd had to restrain a natural impulse to belt him over the head with her shoulderbag. 'I'm sorry,' she'd said icily. 'I'm waiting for my husband.'

She'd dealt with the second one in similar fashion, watched him scurry away to try his luck elsewhere, then shuddered. She'd never have believed that such respectable-looking men could be so disgusting.

Another taxi drawing up at the entrance opposite caught her attention and she saw the doorman step smartly towards it. The rear door opened and a man stepped out. She narrowed her eyes in triumph. It was him!

Her heart began racing and she felt tense with a strange mixture of excitement and trepidation. Even from this distance he presented an unmistakable figure. Immaculately dressed in white dinner jacket and dark trousers, tall, with power and animal grace in every movement of his lithe body. Her mouth was dry now. If only old Morag's prediction had been true. If only he'd loved her with his heart and not just his body. But he hadn't. He had no heart. He was a liar. He was a self-centred, deceitful, cruel and wanton hollow excuse for a man.

Like the gentleman he was pretending to be, he was gallantly offering his arm to his companion as she got out. She was tall and slim with long dark hair. Ruthlessly Catriona suppressed a twinge of jealousy. She should be feeling sorry for her. Perhaps she too had her dreams.

She tightened her lips resolutely. Ten minutes would be long enough. By then they'd be settled at their table, gazing into each other's eyes over the candlelit crystal and silver. Then she'd make her appearance and Mr Ryan Hind could wave goodbye to his reputation for good.

'Good evening, miss.'

She turned her attention wearily to the man who'd stopped and sidled up to her. Not another one, surely!

'Are you talking to me?'

He was too busy leering and ogling her figure to be put off by the cold abruptness in her voice, and he leaned closer and murmured, 'There's a warm little wine bar round the corner. Would you care to join me for a couple of drinks?'

It was pathetic, she thought. He probably had a wife, a couple of kids, and a half-paid mortgage. Well, at least it proved that she looked the part. But could she really act the part? Now was as good a time as any to find out.

With a flutter of her false eyelashes and a provocative smile she spoke to him in a low, husky voice.

'I have expensive tastes, dearie. Can you afford champagne?'

'The best.' He smirked and patted the pocket where presumably he kept his wallet. 'You'll find me very generous. Anything you want.'

She placed a hand on her hip, gave him a smouldering smile and murmured, 'Well, that's all right, then. I adore men who like spending money.' This was too easy, she thought. Best of all, she didn't feel the least bit embarrassed. This clown was ready to believe anything. 'My name's Trixie,' she breathed. 'What's yours?'

'Freddie. Just call me Freddie.' He glanced around nervously. 'Shall we…er…go now?'

Now he was worried in case anyone recognised him. Good, she thought. Make the randy goat suffer. 'Well…that depends on what you have in mind besides buying me a drink, Freddie,' she prompted in her best low and sultry voice.

He tried a lewd, suggestive wink. 'I know a small hotel near here. They're very understanding about these things. We can take a couple of bottles with us and…enjoy ourselves in private.'

She gave him a provocative smile and murmured, 'What do you mean by…"enjoying" ourselves, Freddie?'

He blinked in surprise and looked around nervously once more. She was only playing this by ear and it was clear that her questions were making him suspicious. But she had to persist because she already knew how she was going to deal with this pest and that meant that she had to trick him into saying what he really wanted.

Ensnaring him with another smouldering look, she

teased him. 'You're a very naughty man, Freddie. You really want to take me to bed, don't you? Are you sure you'll make it worth my while?'

'Of course I will,' he insisted, sounding breathless with anticipation. 'I told you I was very generous, didn't I?'

'Yes, Freddie, you did indeed.' Suddenly she switched off her smile and her voice became brisk with authority. 'Perhaps the judge will take that into consideration, but I doubt it.' She patted her shoulder bag. 'If you want to see my warrant card I'll be glad to oblige. I am Woman Police Constable Jordan of the Metropolitan Police vice squad. You will be charged with importuning for an immoral purpose.'

His face collapsed and turned a sickly grey. 'I...I did n-n-nothing. I...I was only...'

'Save your breath,' she snapped coldly. 'You picked the wrong night, Freddie. The squad has this whole area under surveillance by closed circuit television cameras.' The adrenaline was really pumping now and she was enjoying this. Perhaps she was a better actress than she'd thought. Freddie seemed convinced enough that she was the genuine article. It was just a pity that these new shoes were pinching her toes.

'Now then, Freddie...' she went on briskly. 'You're the fourth one we've caught in the last half-hour. The van will be along shortly to pick you up with the others. Until it arrives you will stand in this doorway, facing inwards. I have to report to our temporary headquarters across the road. I must warn you that if you attempt to leave this doorway you will be instantly arrested and further charged with attempting to escape. Just remember that you are being constantly monitored by our cameras.'

Freddie looked positively ill with worry. 'W-will this appear in the newspapers?'

'I wouldn't be surprised if it's on the television news tomorrow,' she replied disdainfully. 'I hope it teaches you to behave yourself from now on.'

She waited until he was obediently facing the door, then with a final warning about attempting to escape she left him and crossed the busy road towards the restaurant.

Without feeling conceited, she was rather proud of her performance. She'd certainly put the fear of God into that creep, and with any luck he'd still be there shivering in his shoes until two in the morning, waiting to be arrested.

Some day, no doubt, she'd look back on this evening's work and wonder at her sheer audacity. The sweet innocence of youth was well and truly lost now. Life in London had seen to that. On the bright side, however, her success with Freddie had given her more confidence for the task ahead.

The first hurdle to negotiate was the doorman, and she could tell from the look of alarm and outrage on his face as she headed for the entrance that he had no intention of allowing a trollop like her to defile the sanctified interior of Cardini's restaurant.

He moved his bulk to bar her way and said sternly, 'I'm sorry, miss. Unaccompanied...' He looked her up and down, as if searching for a suitable description, then sneered, '*Females* are not allowed in. If you want to eat I suggest that you look for a hamburger stall.'

Madge had anticipated this and worked out a solution.

Heaving a sigh and giving a self-conscious smile, Catriona nodded. 'I was afraid of this. I...I do look too much the part in these clothes, don't I? But the fact is that it's only a costume. You see, I'm a student and I make ends meet by working part-time for a kiss-ogram agency. Mr Ryan Hind is dining here tonight, I believe. It's his birthday and his colleagues hired me to deliver birthday wishes along with a rather expensive present to show the regard in which they hold him.'

The doorman's expression was turning from antagonism to uncertainty, and she undermined him further by sighing again. 'Your attitude is quite understandable, of course. Rules are rules, I suppose. I'll just have to go back and tell them that I was quite rightly denied admittance. They'll be terribly disappointed...as will Mr Hind when he finds out. But there we are. It can't be helped. You're only doing your job, aren't you?'

She turned to go but the doorman cleared his throat and said uncomfortably, 'I beg your pardon, miss. I was under a misapprehension. Mr Hind is, of course, a very valued customer. I'm sure I can make an exception in your case.' He tipped his hat and opened the door for her.

She'd expected to have to go through the whole charade again for the benefit of the head waiter when she entered the main restaurant, but it proved unnecessary. He was over on the far side of the room with his back towards her as he discussed the menu with two diners. She knew exactly where to look for her quarry and there he was, just as she'd expected, at his private table talking animatedly with his companion as he poured two glasses of wine. She was about to launch herself across the room at him when she paused and recalled Madge's advice.

'There's no use just *walking* through the room,' she'd said. 'You have to make an entrance. You want to make yourself the focus of everyone's attention, my dear. Every eye in the place must be riveted on you when you confront him.'

'And how do I do that?' she'd asked doubtfully.

'Well, the one thing you don't do is be Catriona McNeil impersonating someone else. That won't fool anyone. You have to become Trixie Trotter. You have to get under her skin and understand what makes her tick. That's the only way to convince an audience.'

'How?' she'd asked again.

'That's up to you. She'll be your creation. Just remember that Trixie doesn't have to be an absolute slut just because she earns her living on the streets. These girls do it out of necessity, not pleasure. Perhaps her husband deserted her, leaving her with two kids and a widowed mother to support. They all live in a run-down council house and the old mother fondly thinks that her daughter has a well-paid job as a cocktail waitress in a West End club. Trixie is saving every penny she earns so that her kids can have a better start in life than she had. Her life on the streets has made her tough and cynical, but she's still got time to feed any stray cat that comes her way.'

Remembering that advice now, Catriona rested one hand on her shoulder bag, placed the other on her hip, thrust out her chest and began a sinuous, figure-flaunting saunter between the tables.

There were immediate gasps and outraged whispers from behind her. Someone coughed and spluttered over a drink and there was a clatter as someone else dropped a knife. A waiter, tray of drinks in hand, gazed at her open-mouthed as she fluttered her eye-lashes at him in passing.

The buzz of conversation was growing louder, and she was only a few feet from the table when Ryan glanced up. Their eyes locked, and as the light played over the classical lines and planes of his face she was again smitten by the full impact of his animal magnetism. But now she could ignore it because she knew what lay beneath.

Apart from an expression of mild curiosity he seemed perfectly composed and at ease with the world, which was more than could be said for his lady-friend, who somehow managed to look curious and alarmed at the same time as it dawned on her that this apparition was coming to *their* table.

There was a pool of expectant silence around the scene as people turned in their seats and craned their necks, waiting with bated breath to see what was going to happen next.

A part of Catriona was on the edge of panic. Like an actress with first-night nerves she wanted to flee the stage before she made a fool of herself, but she fought it down. She was in the grip of something stronger than fear. Some subconscious imperative which was urging her onwards to complete the task she'd come to do.

She glided and undulated to a stop at the table, thrust out a shapely hip, then with one hand still on her waist she raised the other and chastened him with a wagging forefinger. 'Ryan Hind, you are a very, very naughty man.' Her voice was loud and brassy enough to be heard halfway across the room. 'You did it again, didn't you? You left without leaving my usual fee this afternoon, didn't you? When I woke up after our little nap I found that you'd already dressed and gone. And there was no sign of the usual cheque or envelope to be found anywhere in the flat. I mean…how is a working girl expected to pay the rent?'

He stared up at her in stony silence, but she imagined she saw a hint of anger in the grey depths of his eyes. It only lasted a second or two, then he turned his head away and took a casual sip at his drink.

His display of indifference came as an unpleasant surprise, but she was by no means finished with him yet.

Venting a loud sigh of patience she addressed his companion. 'He's always doing that. I'm just giving you a warning, dear. Keep your eye on him. Mind you, it's not because he's tight-fisted or hates to part with his money. None of the girls would ever accuse him of that. I mean…' She made a sweeping gesture with her hand. 'Have you any idea what they charge for a meal in a place like this? My God! I wish all my gentleman friends were as generous as Ryan here.' She flashed him a smile of tolerant forgiveness. 'It's just that he keeps forgetting little things like paying you. It isn't his fault. He's always so busy making all that money, dear. Clients to see…lawyers to consult… As I told him only this afternoon as he was undressing, I often wonder how he gets it all in!'

The girl stared up at her in dismay and horror, her mouth twitching soundlessly, then she hissed across the table, 'Ryan! Do you…do you actually *know* this…this person?'

Catriona squealed with laughter as if she'd just heard the funniest joke in her life. 'Does he know me?

That's a good one, that is! I'm Trixie Trotter. Everyone knows me. Ryan and me has been the best of friends for ages—haven't we, Ryan? You tell her. Why, I was only sixteen at the time, and you was one of my very first clients, weren't you?'

He regarded her in bleak, scornful silence for a moment, then he said in a quiet, menacing voice, 'I don't know who you are, Miss Trotter, but you've had your fun, so run along now like a good girl and stop annoying us or you may have cause to regret it.'

She ignored the chilling threat and made a great show of appearing hurt before bursting into laughter. 'Oh…you're a real tease Ryan, and no mistake. You really are. Always good for a laugh.' Giving him a wicked smile, she pulled a pair of gaudy boxer shorts from her bag and held them up. 'You left these in the flat last week, remember? You'll forget your trousers one of these days. Anyway, I've washed and ironed them for you as usual.' She held them higher, so that everyone could get a good look. 'Aren't they gorgeous?' she remarked to the girl. 'Bright red with little yellow teddy bears. And he's got a pair with dolphins and another pair with little green frogs. I think he's just a big baby at heart.'

There was a series of flashes and she dropped the shorts in his lap and pouted her lips. 'Oh, hell! Someone is taking pictures. I hope my old mum down in Hackney doesn't see them.'

His mouth remained grimly closed but she could feel his scalpel-sharp eyes trying to penetrate her disguise. Her own eyes flashed back in triumph and she longed to rip off the ridiculous wig and remove the false eyelashes and make-up. She longed to see the look on his face when he found out who she really was, but that would have made this well-planned scheme a waste of time. Anyway, it was time to make a strategic withdrawal. All the commotion had finally caught the attention of the head waiter across the room, and he was striding over to find out the cause.

She treated Ryan to one final mocking smile, then saucily made her way through the open-mouthed and astonished diners towards the exit.

As she left the warmth of the foyer and stepped outside onto the pavement the chill in the air made her shiver. The doorman grinned. 'Well, miss? How did you fare in there? Did Mr Hind appreciate his birthday surprise?'

She smiled. 'To tell the truth he didn't say very much. He was certainly surprised, and I think he may have been too overcome with emotion to express how he really felt.'

'As long as he was happy, miss. At Cardini's we pride ourselves on giving our customers an enjoyable evening.'

'I'm sure you do. And I'm sure Mr Hind has had an evening he won't forget in a hurry. Now, could you please call me a cab?'

He whistled one up from the nearby rank, opened the rear door for her and tipped his hat as she handed him a pound coin from her bag. Then she told the driver her address, settled back in her seat and smiled to herself in satisfaction. She'd done it! She'd actually carried it off! And she could hardly wait to get back to the flat and tell Madge.

As the taxi drew away from the kerb she glanced across the road and saw Freddie, still standing nervously in the shop doorway. Men! she thought with contempt. They were all the same. Well, tonight she'd taught two of them a lesson.

Ryan Hind would know now how it felt to be humiliated. When the pictures that had been taken appeared in the newspaper he'd be the laughing-stock of London society and no girl in her right mind would ever dare be seen in his company again.

With a feeling of relief she took off the candyfloss wig and allowed her own golden-red hair to tumble down around her face.

CHAPTER FIVE

THE picture appeared in the following day's evening paper and Madge eyed it with relish then read out the headline. '''Definitely not on the menu at Cardini's.''' She held the paper closer and read out the small print. '''Miss Trixie Trotter, self-confessed street girl, washes dirty linen in top London restaurant. Her alleged client, Mr Ryan Hind, had no comment to make when asked about her allegation that he owed her money for 'services rendered'.'''

Catriona had already seen it, and she gave a bitter smile across the table. 'They're damned right he had no comment to make. Who'd have believed him, anyway? Certainly not the girl he was with. She was turning blue and looked ready to throw a fit when I last saw her. I suppose I feel a bit sorry for causing her embarrassment, but that couldn't be helped, could it?' She sipped her coffee, then added, 'Take my word for it, Madge, it'll be a long, long time before Mr Casanova Hind ever dares show his face there again.'

Madge was still studying the picture closely. Finally she nodded in satisfaction and tossed the paper aside. 'Well, you seem to have done the business on him, all right. And you're absolutely sure that he had no idea who you were?'

'None whatsoever. How could he, beneath that disguise? You said yourself that my own mother wouldn't have known me.'

'And you're sure that you didn't say anything…let

anything slip…or give the least little hint—anything which might have helped him to make the connection?'

Catriona laid down her cup and frowned. Why all the questions? she wondered. And why did Madge suddenly sound so worried? Anyway, it was over and done with now. 'What's wrong?' she demanded. 'Look, I don't give a penny toss if he does discover that it was me. He can't do anything worse to me than he's already done, can he?'

Madge picked up her coffee, then said briskly, 'You've had a trying time lately, my dear. When we first discussed this idea I warned you that you might have to leave London until the dust had settled down, and now I think you really should.'

'What dust?' she asked suspiciously.

Madge smiled and said evasively, 'Be sensible. You've earned yourself a holiday. Take a few weeks off and go and visit your parents in Scotland. I'm sure they've been missing you.'

'What dust?' she asked again, her blue eyes challenging the older woman. Madge lit a cigarette. She'd just put one out a minute ago and that was a sure sign that she had something on her mind. At last she said, 'You've really let the air out of Ryan Hind's tyres, and you can bet your life that he'll pull out all the stops to find out who Trixie really was and if he does—'

'To hell with him!' Catriona snapped. 'I told you…I don't care if he does.'

'Even if he tries to drag you into court?' Madge asked quietly.

Catriona blinked, then took a deep breath and looked at her evenly. 'How could he do that? I didn't

do anything illegal, did I? If you remember, I asked
you right at the start if…'

'Well…not in the usual sense. You wouldn't really
call it illegal,' Madge hedged uncomfortably. 'But
Ryan Hind might well be the vindictive type. He
could feel he has the right to bring a civil action
against you for slander.'

She stared at Madge in silence, then gave a snort
of contempt. 'A lot of good that would do him. If he
took me to court I'd tell them exactly why I did it.
He'd be exposed for the kind of rotten scoundrel he
really is. An unscrupulous, lying, deceitful seducer of
innocent women.'

'Seduction, unfortunately, isn't a civil offence—
whereas slandering a man's reputation is,' Madge said
wearily. 'And let's not forget that he's rich enough to
afford the best lawyer money can buy. I know it isn't
fair, but that's the kind of world we have to live in.'

Catriona's shoulders slumped. This wasn't the best
of news but there was no use blaming Madge. She
should have been able to foresee the consequences for
herself. Undaunted, she sat up straight and said
stoutly, 'I still don't give a damn. Let him do his
worst.'

Madge looked at her thoughtfully. 'If it ever did
get to court it might reach the national newspapers.
Your parents read them, I suppose?'

Damn it! She'd never thought of that!

'Now look,' Madge said soothingly, 'none of this
is likely to happen. It's a worst case scenario. But my
point is this…why take chances? You've had your
revenge on him so get back into the trench and keep
your head down. Anyway, a break from here and a
change of scenery will do you a world of good.' She

gave an encouraging smile. 'Just think of all that lovely fresh air up in Scotland. Take a month off. I'll take on another part-timer until all this blows over and then you can come back.' She glanced at her watch. 'It's only seven-thirty. You've plenty of time to pack a case and catch the night train from King's Cross.'

Catriona sighed. 'Well...if you really think I should. But don't think that I'm running away from him. He doesn't frighten me. I'm only doing this to please you.'

A smile of relief passed over Madge's face. 'Good. Now, you've plenty of nice new clothes to show off to the folks back home, so I'll give you a hand to get packed, then we'll order a taxi.'

Instead of taking the train all the way to Inverness, which would have meant her having to stay there for two days waiting for the twice-weekly bus to Kindarroch, she changed at Glasgow and caught the train to Oban, a busy fishing port on the west coast.

At Oban she went straight down to the harbour and hitched a lift north on one of the fishing boats, which dropped her off at Kindarroch late the following evening.

Her parents, of course, were surprised and delighted to see her and she spent the rest of the night answering their questions and telling them about the wonderful job she had...about Madge...about the luxurious flat she was staying in... But, naturally enough, not a word about Ryan Hind or her recent escapade. They'd have been shocked and scandalised, and would probably have nailed her feet to the floor so that she couldn't go back.

She spent the following day looking up her friends, but she made a point of steering clear of old Morag. From now on her life was going to be in her own hands, and not influenced by well-meaning old fortune-tellers.

On the second morning the sun was blazing down from a cloudless blue sky. The idle fishermen down by the harbour wall looked to the horizon and sniffed the air and all agreed that they were in for a long spell of hot weather.

That was all the encouragement she needed to spend the day swimming at her favourite spot. She filled a Thermos, packed a few sandwiches along with her swimming costume, and headed for the little sandy cove three miles up the coast.

The day passed pleasantly, with dips in the invigorating surf followed by long periods just lying on the silver-coloured sand basking in the sun. Memories of Ryan Hind were slowly beginning to fade. Madge had been right with her advice and about the method of getting him out of her system. By the time she returned to London he'd be just an unpleasant memory, like the time she'd caught mumps as a child.

At five in the evening she took one last dip, then stripped off her swim suit and gave herself a brisk rub-down with the towel before dressing and setting off home.

In Kindarroch, where the locals drove around in beaten up old pick-up trucks or rusty vans, the sight of a gleaming expensive-looking sports car caused more than a passing interest—and more so to her, when she saw it drawn up outside her house.

Wondering who on earth could be paying them a visit, she walked into the living room. Her mouth dropped open in disbelief and her blood froze in her veins. It couldn't be! It wasn't possible!

'Catriona!' said her mother, beaming a smile at her. 'Isn't this a surprise? A friend of yours from London has driven all that way just to see you.'

The grey eyes held a sardonic gleam as Ryan Hind got to his feet with a smile. 'Hello, Catriona. You've no idea how pleased I am to see you again.'

Too dumbstruck to answer, she could only stand and stare at him until her mother bade her sit down at the table to join them. Then, as if from a distance, she heard her father say, 'Ryan here has been telling us all about the wonderful evening you both spent at that grand restaurant in the West End.'

'Cardini's,' Ryan drawled. He smiled innocently at her across the table. 'I'm sure you remember that first evening, Catriona. In fact we met there a second time, didn't we?'

She was over her initial shock now, and she began to get her wits together. She clenched her fists beneath the table and eyed him bleakly. 'Did we?'

He laughed in amusement. 'Of course we did. How could you forget it? You'd been at a fancy dress ball and you were wearing a blonde wig and a rather be-guiling outfit in open lacework. You must remember.'

Well, that settled one question at least. He'd found out who Trixie Trotter had been. God alone knew how, but that could wait for later. The main question was, how had he known to find her here? Madge would never have told him in a hundred years. Had she told him herself? She had a vague memory of him asking where she came from and she had answered... But surely he would never have remembered...

'Ryan tells us he's in the property development business,' her father said conversationally. He laughed at the very idea. 'I've told him that there's no property worth developing in Kindarroch. This is the place time forgot.'

'Well, you'd be surprised,' answered Ryan with an air of confidence. 'I'll be staying at the hotel for a few days.' He smiled at her blandly. 'What I really need is someone to show me around the whole area. I'm sure that since we're such good friends you wouldn't mind doing that, would you, Catriona?'

Her mother spoke up for her. 'Why, of course she wouldn't, Ryan. She'd love nothing better. Isn't that right, Catriona?'

You could see she was impatient and wondering why her daughter was acting so stand-offish. Here was this handsome young man, well off, by the looks of the car he was driving, well-mannered and so obviously keen on her and she hadn't even smiled at him once since she'd come in!

Catriona had no idea what his game was, but until she found out she would just have to go along with it. Feeling sick, but forcing a smile to her lips, she said, 'I don't mind. After all, I'm on holiday, and there isn't much else to do around here, is there?'

Ryan grinned, but only she could see the sardonic twist to his mouth. 'You're surely not bored, Catriona! A girl with your talents? I know for a fact that you're quite a good actress. Isn't there a local rep company you can join?'

The remark was lost on her parents, but she knew she was going to have to get him out of this house where she could demand to know just what the hell he thought he was playing at.

'As soon as you've finished your tea I'll walk you

down to the hotel,' she said, stiffly polite. 'We can talk about the places you want to see on the way.'

'That's a good idea,' grinned Ryan. 'But there's no hurry. Your mother was telling me all about you just before you arrived. It seems that you were quite a handful when you were at school. Always getting yourself into scrapes of one sort or another.'

She eyed him stonily, her hands still clenched in her lap and a knot of anger in her stomach. 'I was no worse than anyone else, Mr Hind. Mothers tend to exaggerate.'

'Not in your case, I imagine,' he said with a thin smile. 'Perhaps it's that lovely red hair of yours. You know what they say about redheads, don't you?'

Her eyes regarded him icily. 'No, I'm afraid I don't. What do they say about redheads, Mr Hind?'

Her mother broke in. 'She gets that red hair from her father. Would you like another buttered scone, Ryan?' As she offered him the plate she shot Catriona a look of parental disapproval.

Catriona ignored it and wondered again how on earth he'd managed to unmask her. He definitely had not recognised her through her disguise so someone must have told him. She could confidently rule out Madge, so who else did that leave? No one as far as she could see. In fact no one else but Madge and herself had known. Anyway, what did it matter how he'd found out? The unpleasant fact was that he was here and there was damn all she could do about it. What she had to worry about now was what he had in mind. She could see nothing ahead but trouble and possible disgrace for both herself and her family.

'You'll be finding it very strange up here after living in London, Ryan,' her father said.

Ryan, looking as relaxed and comfortable as if the place belonged to him, smiled easily. 'Not so strange, Mr McNeil. I spent six months at Assynt after I left university.'

Her father looked at him in surprise. 'That's wild MacLeod country. The Army does a lot of secret training there.'

'Yes...so I believe. These scones are really delicious, Mrs McNeil. I'd forgotten what real home cooking tasted like. I congratulate you.'

'Catriona is a very good cook,' her mother said quickly. 'Perhaps you'll have a chance to sample it before you go back to London. I hear the food in the hotel is not up to much. They haven't got a real chef because they don't get that many visitors, even in the summer.'

Catriona clenched her teeth. Her mother would be offering the wretch the spare room in a minute. She was going to have to have a long talk with her and tell her that Ryan Hind was definitely not her type.

Ryan gave her a mocking grin, then said gravely, 'If her cooking is as good as her other accomplishments I'll look forward to it.'

'And how exactly did you and Catriona meet?' her father asked him, sounding too much like a dutiful parent quizzing a prospective son-in-law for her liking.

'We met quite by accident,' Ryan declared airily. 'You might say that Catriona literally fell into my arms. We had a drink together...then I invited her out to dinner that evening and we became...' his eyes mocked her coldly '...quite friendly, didn't we, Catriona?'

She bit back on the comment she wanted to make

and had to make do with nodding her head and trying not to look too surly about it. To think that her life had been made so miserable all because of an idiot rollerskating on the pavement. It was enough to make you weep, it really was.

'Well, I'm only relieved that it was respectable company such as yourself that she met,' her mother twittered. 'You hear so many stories about young girls going to London on their own and getting involved with the wrong kind of people, getting themselves into all sorts of trouble. Well, I'm sure you know what I mean, Mr Hind.'

'Indeed I do, Mrs McNeil,' he said with feeling. 'Like all great cities, London has its fair share of disreputable characters who are only too quick to take advantage of the young and innocent girls who flock there looking for adventure.'

Catriona glared at him. She couldn't sit here and take much more of this in silence, she told herself desperately. He'd already made a fool of her. Was he intent now on making a fool of her parents as well?

'It so happens, Mr Hind, that I did meet one particularly nasty piece of work in London,' she said coldly. She realised the risk she was running in alerting and arousing the curiosity of her parents, but she went on regardless. 'I'm sure you know the kind of creature I'm talking about. The type of man who'll lie and cheat and say anything just to get his way.'

Her mother looked at her sharply. 'I hope you sent him packing with a flea in his ear.'

Ryan laughed. 'I don't think you need to worry on that score, Mrs. McNeil. I'm sure that your daughter is more than capable of looking after herself. She's quite a resourceful young lady.' He grinned at Catriona. 'You did send him packing, didn't you?'

Her blue eyes blazed away at him, but she managed to keep the bitterness from her voice when she replied, 'Oh…he had me fooled for a while, but when I found out the truth about him I got my own back.'

'Good for you,' he said with approval. 'Let's just hope that's the last you'll hear of him. Some people can be very persistent, especially when they feel they have a score to settle.' He turned to her mother innocently. 'May I prevail upon you for another cup of your excellent tea, Mrs McNeil?'

Catriona watched in despair as her mother almost fell over herself in her eagerness to please him. How long had he said he intended staying in Kindarroch? A few days? That story he'd spun her father about his reason for coming here had been nothing but his usual lies. Only she knew the real reason, which was to exact retribution on her. So why didn't he just leave it to his damned lawyers? She might be able to cope with that, but not this. Did he intend tormenting her, playing her like a fish on the end of a line until he was ready for the kill?

For the sake of her parents she kept a strained smile on her face, but it was put severely to the test when her mother went to the sideboard and returned proudly with a photograph album.

'Mother!' she cried in despair. 'No. Please. I'm sure Mr Hind doesn't have the time for that.'

'Och, don't be so silly, Catriona.' her mother chided. 'You were a bonnie wee girl. I'm sure Mr Hind would like to see some of the photographs we took.' Opening the album, she placed it in front of

Ryan. 'Now, here she is when she was only three years old...'

Catriona gave a silent groan and slumped in her chair.

The album wasn't that big, but you could have read the complete works of Shakespeare in the time it took her mother to go through it. Every picture was studied and discussed in detail... when it was taken, where it was taken, who had knitted the jumper she was wearing, who the people in the background were... The only thought Catriona found cheering was that Ryan Hind might drop dead of boredom, but he didn't. Being the experienced liar and actor that he was, he gave the impression of being utterly absorbed until the album was finally closed and locked back in the drawer where it belonged.

Ryan finally got to his feet and she watched him with a jaundiced eye. He certainly believed in dressing for the occasion, she thought. No one in the Highlands wore smart business suits, and at the moment he was wearing a dark blue Harris tweed jacket over a white shirt—though what right he had to be wearing a Stewart tartan tie she didn't know. The Stewart clan would have disclaimed any responsibility for bringing a knave like him into the world.

'You're surely not going yet?' her mother protested. She turned to her husband. 'Father, where's your sense of hospitality? You haven't even offered Mr Hind a glass of whisky yet.'

Catriona groaned again. If her father brought the bottle out this could go on for hours! Getting to her own feet, she looked at her mother pointedly and said, 'I'm sure Mr Hind has work to do. And I promised to walk him back to the hotel so that we can talk about the places he wants to see. I'd like to do that before it gets too late.'

Ryan grinned. 'Catriona is quite right. You've been more than kind and I'm sure we'll meet again before I return to London.'

When the goodbyes had been said and they were outside, she waited until they were out of sight of the house before halting and rounding on him furiously. 'All right, Mr Hind, just what the hell are you doing here?'

He smiled at her grimly and pretended to be surprised. 'Do you give all your visitors such a cold reception? And here was I thinking that you'd be overjoyed to see me again.'

'Don't mess about with me, you bastard,' she snapped. 'You might have fooled my parents but I know you for the snake that you are.'

There was a flash of brittle anger in his eyes, then he commented dryly, 'You've changed. Prettier than ever, I may say, but there's a rough edge to your tongue which wasn't there before. And I suggest you keep your voice down unless you want the whole village to overhear our friendly little conversation.'

She glared at him angrily and hissed, 'You're a despicable creature. Don't think for one moment that I'm afraid of the likes of you.'

A dark brow rose in a scornful disbelief. 'Aren't you? Then why did you leave London?'

'That's none of your damned business.' She poked him in the chest with her forefinger. 'I'm warning you. You stay away from my parents. They're decent, honest people. I realise that you don't know the meaning of decency and honesty, but nevertheless I'm telling you not to come back here again.'

Before she could react he'd grabbed her wrist, and she found herself imprisoned in his arms. Looking up at him furiously, she gasped, 'Let me go, you heathen!' She tried to kick his shins but she couldn't get her foot high enough.

'Quite the little wildcat, aren't you?' he said with derision. 'It must be something they have in the water up here. You were a lot friendlier than this when we first met in London. It didn't take much persuasion to get you into bed, as I recall. You seemed to be all for it.'

She struggled in vain to free herself, and, seething with fury and frustration, she spat the words at him. 'I didn't know what kind of low-life you were then, did I? Now, if you don't let me go this instant I'll—'

Before she got the chance to finish she was almost jerked off her feet as he yanked her closer and crushed his mouth down onto hers. Numbed with shock and the sheer audacity of the man, she could do nothing but endure the bruising assault until it was over, leaving her dizzy and fighting for breath.

'At least the lips are still as sweet and tender,' he observed with grim humour. 'I'm looking forward eagerly and with great impatience to find out about the rest of your sweet and delicious little body.'

She could hardly credit her ears, and she grated through her clenched teeth, 'You'll have to wait till hell freezes over in that case.'

He let her free from his imprisoning arms and said smoothly, 'Oh, I don't think it'll take as long as that, Catriona. I've a feeling that whether you want to or not you're going to be very co-operative in the matter.' He grinned. 'Who knows? You may even enjoy it as much as you did the last time.'

He was unbelievable! And he looked so sure of himself that for a moment she found herself wondering... 'In your dreams,' she scoffed. She dusted herself down, as if to free herself of any contamination, then she narrowed her eyes at him and said quietly, 'You must be mad. You're taking a chance showing your face around here, you know. I've got at least a dozen cousins and uncles between here and Oban. You could easily find yourself being used for lobster bait if they hear what you did to me.'

He dismissed her threat with a nonchalant shrug. 'I doubt it. Now if I'd taken you against your will that would be different, but, as I've already said, far from putting up a struggle you were more than eager to make free with your not inconsiderable charms.'

She tossed her hair angrily out of her eyes and began walking towards the harbour. 'You tricked me,' she muttered. 'You deliberately led me on and made me believe that...that...' Her voice faltered, then she snapped, 'You know what I'm talking about. Don't try to deny it.'

'I haven't denied anything yet,' he reminded her sourly. 'And don't threaten me again. You're in enough trouble as it is. I'm the injured party around here, not you. Just remember that in future.'

'*You're* the injured party! You mean that just because I—' She broke off in mid-sentence as she saw the Reverend McPhee waddling up the road towards them. 'Here's the minister coming,' she whispered fiercely. 'You're a stranger here and he'll be wondering who you are so I'll have to tell him something. Don't you dare say a word. You just keep your mouth shut and let me do the talking.'

He taunted her with a sardonic smile. 'Why? Are

you scared that I might turn the tables on you and ruin your reputation as you tried to ruin mine? Afraid he'll find out that one of his little lambs has gone astray?'

She swallowed her anger and pinned a bright smile to her face as the minister approached. 'Good evening, Minister,' she said cheerfully.

'And a good evening to you, Catriona.' It didn't matter whether he was conducting a funeral or a christening, his voice never changed. Always sorrowful and laden with doom. He eyed Ryan mournfully and she introduced him hurriedly.

'This is Mr Hind from London. He can't speak at the moment. The poor man has a terrible case of laryngitis. He's under strict instructions from his doctor to rest his voice.'

'Is that so…? Well, tell him I'm sorry to hear that, Catriona. Tell him I hope he gets better soon. I often get a sore throat myself after a sermon on the Sabbath and I find a wee touch of honey in warm milk works wonders.'

It was time he retired, she thought. He was getting past it. 'You can tell him yourself, Minister,' she said politely. 'I didn't say he was deaf. He just can't talk.'

'Aye…just so.'

'He's up here on business, Minister. He deals in property. I'm just showing him around.'

'Aye…well…it's nice to have you back among your own kind, Catriona. There are too many young people who leave here only to succumb to the vices and temptations of the big city. But I've been praying for you and I can see that it hasn't been in vain. Sin always leaves its mark, but you are as yet untouched. You're a credit to Kindarroch and your parents.'

'Well, that's very kind of you, Minister,' she murmured, managing not to turn scarlet with shame. 'I try my best.'

She heaved a sigh of relief when the encounter was over and Ryan grinned. 'Does he always talk like that?'

'What if he does?' she challenged frostily. 'He's our minister and don't you dare make a fool of him. We like him just the way he is. Anyway, he might be getting old but he's still twice the man you'll ever be.'

'Well, I'm not going to argue about that, but tell me—am I going to catch laryngitis every time we run into company?' he demanded. 'If that's the case I think we should find some place where we can continue our discussion in privacy. We could go to my hotel room and put a ''Do not Disturb'' notice on the door.'

'You've about as much chance of ever getting me in a hotel room again with you as you have of sprouting wings,' she said with feeling. 'We can continue our discussion out on the harbour entrance. We won't be disturbed there.'

Grim-faced and silent, she led the way past the deserted fish market, along the quayside and out onto the granite-built breakwater. The evening sun was turning the unusually calm sea the colour of molten gold and a pair of gulls wheeled in lazy circles overhead. This had been one of her favourite spots as a child. Long, hazy summer days spent barefoot, dangling a piece of string with a shelled mussel and hook on the end into the water below. She'd never caught anything but it had been a good excuse just to sit and dream her childish fantasies. But she'd certainly never dreamed of anything like this.

When they reached the end of the breakwater she stopped, put her hands on her hips and said truculently, 'We have all the privacy we need right here, Mr Hind, so let's get this over and done with. As far as I'm concerned we're even. In fact, if you ask me, you got off lightly. All I want you to do now is to leave me alone. Get back in your car and get out of my life for ever.'

He had hitched one leg up on a bollard and now he regarded her thoughtfully, with knitted brows and folded arms. Finally he shook his head. 'I've no intention of leaving you alone. You've caused me a lot of trouble, Catriona. One way or another you're going to make amends for that, and I'm not leaving Kindarroch until you do.'

She gave a disdainful toss of her head. 'In that case you'd better be prepared to spend the rest of your life here.'

He grinned, flashing two rows of white teeth at her. 'I may be doing that in any case. Since you so successfully ruined my reputation in London I've had to consider the possibility of doing business elsewhere. This sleepy little village has good potential for development. How would you like me as a neighbour?'

She was aghast. He was joking, of course. He had to be. The thought of him living here as a permanent threat and reminder was too much. It had to be an empty threat, just made to frighten her, but she wasn't going to fall for it.

'We could at least be friends...' he suggested with heavy sarcasm. 'Just think about it. We could have social evenings in the hotel bar. You could entertain

the crowd doing your Trixie Trotter impersonation.
I'm sure they've never seen anything like it up here.
You were very good, you know. You played the part
to perfection and you had everyone completely
fooled.'

With an effort she managed to hold onto her temper
and asked him the question which had been rattling
about in her mind since he'd turned up out of the blue.
'If I had you fooled how did you find out it was me?'

He shrugged. 'That was easy enough. The doorman
knew the taxi driver who picked you up. It was simply
a case of waiting until the same driver turned up at
the rank the following evening and asking him where
he'd dropped you off. As soon as he mentioned
Palmerston Court in Chelsea I knew it had been you.
The driver even remembered that you had red hair
when you took the wig off.' He grinned amiably at
her. 'When I went round to the flats to challenge you
the security man in the foyer told me that you'd gone
home to Scotland on holiday. Fortunately I've got a
good memory, and I remembered you telling me the
name of this place.'

Well, so much for that, she reflected dismally.
There was no one to blame but herself. But then she
hadn't been overly concerned about covering her
tracks, had she? At the time she couldn't have cared
less, but now she wished she had.

She chewed worriedly at her lip, then looked at him
defiantly. 'What exactly do you mean by me having
to make amends to you? If it's an apology you're
looking for you can forget it. I'm not in the least bit
sorry for what I did. In fact I'd do it again if I got
the chance.'

His mouth twitched, whether in anger or amusement she wasn't sure, but there was an ominous edge to his voice when he growled, 'An apology is no use to me. You could get down on your hands and knees and kiss my feet for all the good it'll do you. Don't think that you're getting off that easy.'

'I see…' she said stiffly. 'So you're going to take me to court for slander, is that it?' This was what Madge had warned her about. It could mean the court case appearing in the national press.

He laughed again, then shook his head. 'I doubt if that would be worth my while. You wouldn't be much use to me if you were languishing in jail because you couldn't pay the substantial damages the court would award me.'

She was getting a bad feeling about this, and she looked at him suspiciously. 'In that case would you mind telling me what you *do* intend doing?'

The grey eyes looked her over with bold insolence, then he gave her another flash of hungry white teeth. 'Trixie Trotter would have known exactly what I wanted.'

She drew in a shocked breath, then glared at him. 'You're out of your mind. And disgusting with it.'

He looked hurt. 'Now, now, Catriona, be reasonable.' He paused and his eyes hardened again as he subjected her to a caustic scrutiny. 'I'm a man who has grown accustomed to the simple and perfectly natural pleasures of life. On a regular basis, I might add. But thanks to your little exhibition in the restaurant these pleasures have been denied me for the time being. I feel it's only right and proper that until things improve it's up to you to attend to my physical needs. I'm sure you'll agree that's not too much to ask. And after all it's only justice, isn't it?'

You had to marvel at the cold-blooded nerve of the man, she thought. She looked him straight in the eye and said quietly, 'Get lost.'

He shook his head in mock sorrow, then reached for the inside pocket of his jacket and said tiredly, 'That's a very petty attitude to take, Catriona. Of course I thought you might be unreasonable and object to the idea so I took the precaution of bringing this along with me.' With a smile of regret he handed her the folded page of newsprint.

She opened it out and suddenly felt sick as she saw the photograph and the story.

'It's very good, isn't it?' he remarked conversationally. 'Of course, once you know who Trixie really is it's quite easy to see the remarkable resemblance. They don't get the London papers up here, so I don't imagine anyone in the village has seen this yet.'

She glared at him, then turned aside, crumpled the page up and tossed it into the water.

He looked down and watched in silence as the paper slowly disintegrated and sank out of sight, then he shrugged. 'It's a good job I brought extra copies with me. They're in my suitcase back at the hotel.'

Her shoulders slumped and for a moment she stood with her head bowed in despair, then she faced him coldly. 'What do you intend doing with them?'

He went on as if he'd never heard her. 'We'll call it *The Secret Life of Catriona McNeil.* She left Kindarroch to find fame and fortune in London but, like so many others, she became a street-walker. Who'd have thought she'd end up like that? Certainly not the Reverend McPhee! And certainly not her kind, hard-working and God-fearing parents. I dare say it would break their hearts. You could deny it, but I don't think anyone would believe you.' His grey eyes were watching her with bleak amusement. 'Only this afternoon your mother was telling me about the wonderful job you've got…and the flat you're staying in…and all the beautiful clothes you've suddenly acquired. If she saw that picture it would suddenly all make sense to her, wouldn't it?'

'I work in a boutique in Chelsea,' she said dully.

'Of course you do. I believe you, Catriona. But would your mother? Or anyone else for that matter? You more than anyone should appreciate the power of scandal to destroy a reputation. People always like to believe the worst of their neighbours. It makes them feel superior.'

Every word he'd said was true, she acknowledged to herself in misery, and she could no longer bear to look into his eyes. Biting her lip, she looked over the harbour towards the houses and shops. She'd felt safe here with her parents and among her friends. This was her home. All her childhood memories were here. Now this man was going to destroy everything. The only thing she could do now was to sneak away like a thief in the night and find some place to hide. He'd know where to find her if she went back to London, so it would have to be somewhere else, where no one knew her and she could start afresh. Change her name, perhaps?

'You'd really do that, wouldn't you?' she said, her voice tired and bitter with accusation.

'Well, what would you expect from a piece of despicable low-life like me?' He drawled through a crooked grin. 'I've got an image to keep up, haven't I?'

'So, either I…I agree to sleep with you whenever you feel like it or you'll spread these lies about me.'

'That's it in a nutshell,' he agreed with an ironic twist to his lips. 'I couldn't have put it better myself.'

'That's called blackmail,' she said, her blue eyes looking him up and down with contempt. 'You're even viler than I thought.'

He shrugged. 'You can always go to the police if you think it would do any good. But somehow I don't think you will.' He looked up at the gulls circling overhead, then said quietly, ' As for sleeping with me…we'll talk about that later. All I want from you at present is a friendly smile now and again and your promise to show me around the district. Now that I've seen this place I really do think that it needs someone like me to bring it back to life. You have a driving licence, I hope?'

She nodded, eyeing him warily.

'Good.' He stood erect, then tossed his car keys at her. 'My car is still parked outside your house. Kindly bring it down to the hotel after breakfast tomorrow morning.' He turned and strode back along the breakwater in the direction of the hotel, leaving her staring after him in frustrated, toe-curling rage.

Two minutes later he strode into the bar, gave a friendly nod to the handful of locals, then settled himself on a bar stool and ordered a large whisky. Life was full of little surprises, Ryan thought with wry humour. It had been a spur-of-the-moment decision to come here. A decision, he realised now, made in anger. Common sense told him that the most sensible thing to do now was to simply forget the whole thing, spend the night here, then return to London tomorrow.

But for the first time in his life he didn't feel like being sensible.

This Catriona McNeil was entirely different from the one he'd met in London. This was a feisty fire-cracker of a woman who needed to be taught a lesson. Besides that there was something about those big blue eyes which he found intriguing and very hard to resist.

CHAPTER SIX

CATRIONA lay awake most of that night, tossing, turning and only sleeping fitfully, and she had to drag herself out of bed in the morning. Had she had one decent night's sleep since she'd met that man? She couldn't recall any. Her head and limbs felt heavy, but a hot and then a cold shower managed to put some life back into her. She looked out of the window at the weather as she brushed her teeth. It looked as if it was going to be another scorcher of a day so she put on a light cotton skirt and a gaily striped sleeveless blouse, brushed her hair vigorously then wandered into the kitchen and greeted her mother.

'I was going to make breakfast, Mum. I didn't realise anyone was up yet. Now why don't you sit down and let me do that?'

Her mother kept stirring the porridge and said reprovingly, 'It's almost seven o'clock. Living in London has made you soft. When you lived here you were up at six on the dot every morning, like everyone else.' She nodded towards the back door. 'Father's been out there for the last hour mending his lobster pots.'

Catriona poured herself a cup of tea, then perched herself on a seat at the table. If she told her mother that some people in London had to get up at five-thirty just so that they could get to their work on time she'd never have believed her. She wouldn't have believed it herself until she'd gone there and seen the queues for the buses and underground.

'I hope you're in a better mood this morning than you were last night,' her mother said huffily. 'We could hardly get two words out of you. And the face on you was enough to turn the milk sour.'

'I…I'm sorry, Mum,' she muttered in apology. 'I had a headache.'

'Humph!' Her mother wasn't impressed. 'Everyone gets headaches but it's no excuse for bad manners. Your father and I were only trying to make conversation. It's only natural that we're interested in your new friends and the people you've met. We are your parents, after all.'

Catriona sighed. 'I said I was sorry. Now can we just leave it at that, please? The headache isn't quite gone yet.'

'Anyone with half an eye can see that Mr Hind is quite taken with you,' her mother went on, paying no attention to her plea. 'And you could do a lot worse for yourself…'

She tried to shut out the sound as her mother continued her eulogy of Ryan Hind, but it was like trying to ignore a nagging toothache. Mind you, she couldn't really blame her mother. Ryan Hind had that effect on people. Especially women—whatever their age. He had the dark good looks of some fictional romantic hero. Utterly charming…polite…considerate… He seemed to have everything a woman could wish for in a man. He'd even had her fooled, never mind her mother. It was only when it was too late that you discovered the reality under the polished veneer.

If only she had the courage to tell her mother right now how mistaken she was. But that would mean ex-

posing herself and she balked at doing that. She also
had to think of the effect it would have on her parents
if she refused to co-operate with Ryan and he carried
out his threat. They'd be devastated. And even if she
told them the truth they'd still be devastated. She was
trapped in a no-win situation. Damned if she did and
damned if she didn't.

If only Madge were here. Madge had been around
and she'd know how to deal with Ryan Hind and his
outrageous attempt at blackmail. Or even if she didn't
she was bound to know someone who did. But what
on earth would her mother make of Madge, with her
continual smoking and drinking and sometimes fruity
language? She knew what the Reverend McPhee
would say. He'd take one look at Madge and shake
his head dolefully and mutter, 'Now there's a face
filled with broken commandments if ever I saw one.'

Thankfully her mother had never pried too closely
into that particular subject. As far as she knew, Madge
was simply a kind-hearted old dear who owned a shop
and who had offered her the spare room in her flat.

She could always phone Madge, of course, tell her
the situation and ask her advice. She turned that option over in her mind for a moment, then rejected it.
Exploiting a friendship wasn't her style. Madge had
already done more for her than anyone had a right to
expect. Either she dealt with this problem herself or
she had no right to call herself a mature and indepen-
dent adult able to take care of herself.

'Catriona!'

She gave a start. 'Sorry, Mum. I...I was daydreaming.'

'Aye. I can see that. I asked you to go and tell your

father that his breakfast is ready. Make sure he takes his boots off before he comes in the kitchen.'

After breakfast Catriona took over the task of washing the dishes and tidying up. She took her time over it, dragging it out as long as possible. Then she gave her mother a hand with the housework, but by ten everything was finished and she knew she couldn't put it off any longer.

Clutching the keys to Ryan's car, she went outside. The sun had made the interior of the car unbearably hot and she wound down the window and left the car door open for a few minutes. When it had cooled down sufficiently, she eased herself into the driver's seat. She had to adjust it so that her feet could reach the pedals, then she closed the door and turned on the ignition. The engine sprang to life with a throaty purr and she sat for a moment studying the layout of the dashboard. She hadn't a clue what half the dials were for. What did 'tach' mean? You'd need a pilot's licence to take this on the road, she thought. It was a real man's car. It smelt of rich, new leather and pine air freshener. Holding her breath, she depressed the clutch, put her hand on the short, stubby gear lever and selected first gear, then let off the handbrake.

To her astonishment it was much easier to drive than anything she'd ever been in before, and she headed towards the harbour toying with the idea of jumping out at the last minute and letting it coast downhill on its own, straight into twenty feet of water. That would show him exactly how she felt about him and his threats.

She parked outside the hotel, then walked into the bar. 'Good morning, Donnie. Could you let Mr Hind know that I'm here to collect him?'

Donnie the barman, who was restocking the shelves in preparation for lunchtime opening, grinned at her. 'Go up and tell him yourself. He's in the big room at the front.'

Seeing that there was nothing else for it, she climbed the stairs and knocked at the room door.

'Come in,' the deeply, resonant voice commanded.

Squaring her shoulders and taking a deep breath, she opened the door and saw him standing in front of the wardrobe mirror putting on a tie. He turned, and, like a man in a car showroom appraising a new model he was about to acquire, looked her over, then smiled in satisfaction and greeted her affably. 'Good morning, Catriona. You look very pretty in that blouse. Well, don't just stand there. Come in and shut the door behind you.'

She looked at him icily. 'Not for a million pounds. I remember only too well what happened the last time I was in a hotel room with you. I'll wait downstairs by the car until you're ready.' She turned haughtily and went back downstairs.

If he'd felt rebuffed by her action he showed no sign of it when he joined her outside five minutes later. He ran his eyes over her again, only increasing her feeling of discomfort, then he patted the car roof. 'Did you feel comfortable driving it?'

She was leaning against the door with her arms folded and she gave a shrug of studied indifference. 'I managed. It's still in one piece, isn't it?'

'So I see. Right. In that case you can act as my chauffeur.'

'I'm not acting as your anything,' she informed him in a brittle voice. 'You can do your own driving.'

The amiable smile remained on his lips but there

was a sudden chilling glint in his eyes and he said softly, 'There seems to be a lamentable lack of understanding here, Catriona. I thought I'd made your position perfectly clear to you yesterday. Since you seem to have forgotten, I'll take this opportunity to remind you...' For the benefit of any onlookers there might be he gave her a friendly pat on the shoulder and continued, 'While I'm here your only purpose in life is to please me...to satisfy my every whim...and to look happy while you're doing it. If you can't manage that then you'll have to be prepared to face the consequences. Now...have you got that clear in that pretty little head of yours?'

For a moment she glared back at him rebelliously, then she swallowed the bitter bile in her throat and muttered, 'All right...damn you.'

He shook his head sadly. 'That's not good enough, Catriona. The correct response was, "Certainly, Ryan. Anything you say, Ryan."'

Her blue eyes simmered with rage and she hissed, 'Don't push your luck. I might just decide it isn't worth it.'

He studied her a moment longer, weighing her up, challenging her determination, then he nodded. 'You've got fire. Be careful you don't burn yourself.' He opened the front door of the car and gestured at her to get into the driver's seat. 'I want you to drive because you know the roads around here better than I do.'

She could see Donnie watching them from the bar window and she knew the danger of prolonging the argument. If Donnie had any reason to think there was anything amiss it would be common knowledge around the village long before closing time. Then there would be awkward questions. Especially from her mother.

When Ryan had settled his long frame in the front seat he unfolded an Ordnance Survey map of the area, and she asked sulkily, 'Just where exactly is it you want to go? There's nothing but moor, mountains and lochs around here. I hardly think you've got the kind of soul to appreciate good scenery.'

'That only goes to show how little you know of me,' he murmured, engrossed in the map. 'Once you thaw out and get that chip off your shoulder you might get to know me better.'

'The little I do know of you is more than enough, thank you,' she retorted. 'In any case isn't this all a waste of time? You came here for one reason only and it has nothing to do with property development. That was just a cover story for my parents' benefit, so you don't have to keep up the pretence with me.'

He put the map away, then said briskly, 'Fair enough. If that's the way you want it then we could always just go back to my hotel room...'

Her eyes widened in outrage and her tongue got ready to flay him, then she saw the mocking humour in his eyes and she tightened her lips in silent anger.

He laughed at her discomfort, then continued easily, 'You're right, as far as it goes. I only had one thought in my mind when I came here. But when I found out that the hotel was going to be put up for sale my business instincts took over.' He patted her knee affectionately. 'That's no reflection on your obvious attractions. I always keep business and pleasure separate.'

She pushed his hand away and bit her lip. The thought of him getting control of anything in

Kindarroch made her shudder. Never again would she feel comfortable or at home in the village. He would be a permanent blot on the landscape. A reminder of past indiscretion.

'The McLeans have owned that hotel for generations,' she scoffed. 'If they can't make it pay now what chance do you think an outsider like you has got?'

'Fresh ideas?' he offered. 'A willingness to accept that the world is rapidly changing and the know-how to adapt?'

'Oh, well, there's nothing quite so becoming as modesty, they say.'

He ignored the sarcastic remark and pointed through the windscreen. 'That house up on the hill. Do you know who lives there?'

Her eyes followed the direction of his finger and she looked at him sharply, noting the look of strange curiosity on his face. 'Why?' she demanded.

'Because it must have the best view in Kindarroch and I'm interested in it.'

'Well, you'd better get uninterested in it,' she advised caustically. 'That cottage belongs to old Morag and you'd better not fool around with her. She's a witch and she might decide to change you into a worm.' She sniffed, then muttered, 'Mind you, it might be an improvement.'

He continued staring up the hill, as if the sight of the cottage fascinated him, then he grinned at her. 'I'm in the property business, remember? That place could fetch a fortune as a holiday home. Do you think she'd be interested in selling?'

She gave a frosty, satisfied smile. 'Never. You can forget it.'

He tugged at his ear thoughtfully, then drawled, 'Everyone has their price, you know. She can't be very well off, so if I made her a good enough offer....'

'That's typical of people like you, isn't it?' she snapped, then mimicked him, ''Everyone has their price, you know.'' Well, for your information there are some people up here who can't be bought. Morag is one of them. She isn't interested in money. Yours nor anyone else's.'

He gave her an odd, quizzical look, then grunted, 'You seem to know a hell of a lot about her. You could be wrong.'

She shook her head adamantly, then sighed. 'Look...I should just let you go ahead and make a fool of yourself, but I don't want you hassling Morag. She's an old woman and...and she'll live the rest of her life out in that cottage. There's a story about that but an unfeeling brute like you wouldn't understand.'

He kept staring up at the cottage in silence, then he turned to her with a frown. 'I might. Why don't you tell me and let me make up my own mind?'

Well, anything was worth a try, she told herself doubtfully. Hard and callous as this man was, there might be one tiny spark of decency left in his black cinder of a heart. Gazing up at the cottage, she quietly told him all she knew...about how Morag had come from the islands as a young girl and had fallen in love with one of the young fishermen in the village and how he'd died in a storm only two days after the wedding...how she'd kept everything in the house just the way it had been on the day he'd drowned...how she always sat at her window certain that one day Seumus, her husband, would return from the sea which had claimed him.

Fully expecting Ryan to deride and dismiss the story as superstitious nonsense, she was surprised to see the distant look in his grey eyes. He sat for a while, as if brooding over the story, then he said quietly, 'Seumus is Gaelic for James, isn't it?'

She looked at him oddly. 'That's right. Lots of the older ones up here have Gaelic names.'

He kept staring at the cottage and she knew exactly what was going through his mind. How much would Morag settle for and how much could he get in rent if he hired it out as a holiday home to some affluent couple from the south of England? No wonder they called him the Golden Hind. Just a cold, avaricious pirate.

Finally he slung his jacket onto the rear seat and growled, 'OK. Take the road north for about five miles then head inland. And take your time; we're in no hurry.'

He might not be but she was. The sooner this was over and he crept back to his lair in London the better. As she put the car in gear and moved off he turned on the air-conditioning and settled back with an air of relaxed contentment.

The roads up here were all single-track, with well-posted passing places. They were safe enough if you kept your speed down and didn't hurtle round blind corners where you were liable to find yourself facing a juggernaut coming in the other direction. That meant that you had to reverse back and manoeuvre into the passing place you'd just shot by because there was no way the man with the tattooed knuckles was going to reverse *his* vehicle. It was bigger than yours.

The sun was climbing higher into the clear blue sky

and the Western Highlands had never looked lovelier. The glen stretching before them and the towering mountains on either side were painted in hues of gold and green and purple. Over to their left a herd of red deer grazed along the flank of a foothill, and high in the sky ahead of them an eagle hovered, ready to swoop down on some unsuspecting mountain hare browsing through the heather and birch scrub.

In the winter all this could be an icy desolation, where only the foolhardy would venture, but on a day like this it was God's own country and made you pity the poor devils who had to spend their lives in the suffocating confines of a city. The only thing lacking in the midst of all this glory was the opportunity to earn a decent living, Catriona thought sadly. You had to leave it all behind and try your luck elsewhere— and run the risk of becoming involved with people like Ryan Hind.

Her musings came to an end when he said abruptly, 'According to the map there used to be a stately mansion around here. Any idea how to get there?'

'That'll be the old Duke's place. There's no point in going there. It's just a ruin. Half the roof has gone.'

'Nevertheless, I'd still like to see it.' He eyed her provocatively. 'Of course, if there's anything else you'd rather do…?'

She pointed to a large clump of trees about half a mile ahead and said hastily, 'It's there, hidden from view.'

The track leading to the house was slowly but inexorably being reclaimed by nature and was barely visible as it twisted and wound its way through the heavy stand of birch and Scots pine. Finally she drew up and switched off the engine. 'Well, there you are. Don't say I didn't warn you.'

He took a notepad and pen from the glove compartment. 'Don't worry. I won't. Now let's get out and stretch our legs while I look around.'

The house was two storeys high and built of locally quarried granite, and although the door was hanging on by one hinge the windows had been secured and boarded up in days long ago. But, abandoned and neglected as it looked, there was still a sense of solidity and endurance about it. It would still be standing here five hundred years from now.

As he began sketching the various features of the front view she peered over his shoulder, interested in spite of herself.

'Any idea who it belongs to, Catriona?' he asked.

She shrugged. 'The place has been empty for as long as anyone around here can remember. My father once told me that it was built in the last century as a hunting lodge for some duke or other.'

Intrigued, because she'd never actually seen the inside herself, she tagged on behind him as he went and swung the creaking door open. Through the gloom she could see that the walls had been stripped of their panelling and that half the banister rail was missing from the central staircase, but that didn't seem to worry Ryan. He was stamping around the main hallway, testing the soundness of the floor timbers. He went through the whole house like that, taking notes and sketching, then he went outside for a final look.

Finally he gave a grunt of satisfaction. 'It's sound enough. I could have this place restored to its former glory within six months.'

She looked at him as if he was mad. 'And then

what would you do with it?' she queried. 'Not that I care if you want to waste your money, but who, except a hermit, would want to live in a remote place like this? There isn't another living soul for twenty miles around.'

'I'm aware of that, Miss Know-it-all,' he said, with an irritating smile of condescension. 'That could be its main attraction for the purpose I have in mind.'

She nodded sarcastically, as if the truth was just dawning. 'Oh, I know what it'll be. You're going to build a private harem for all your girlfriends. Then you'll surround the place with barbed wire and starving Dobermanns so they can't escape.'

He gave her a long, hard look. He had been puzzled as to her reasons for going to such lengths to ridicule him in public. It had seemed a little over the top to him at the time but it struck him now that she might have been motivated more by jealousy than resentment at the way he'd ditched her.

He found the idea flattering but a little disconcerting. Although he considered jealousy a predominantly female emotion, he'd never encountered it in any of the many women he'd recently been involved with. Women like them just seemed to take it as bad luck and part of the game, and that suited his purposes fine. But this was the first time he'd ever encountered a woman like Catriona McNeil...and perhaps it wasn't before time.

He decided to throw a straw in the wind. Adopting an engaging smile, he said enthusiastically, 'That's an appealing thought, Catriona. But the fence would be to keep others out, so that you and I could spend the winter together. Imagine the roads blocked with snow and the freezing wind howling over the moor. And there we are, snug and warm in front of a roaring log fire…making love on the sheepskin rugs whenever we feel like it…'

His eyes had locked on to hers and it took a tremendous effort of will to look away. They seemed to have the power to paralyse and drain your will. The man was a positive menace, she thought weakly. If she wasn't careful she was going to be ensnared a second time. Giving him a withering look, she said stiffly, 'It'll soon be lunchtime and the nearest place is twenty-five miles from here.'

His eyes remained on hers a moment longer, then he took one last look at the house and surrounding landscape and said crisply, 'OK, let's go. I don't want you accusing me of making you go hungry along with everything else.'

As she got the car going again he studied the map. 'There's a hotel further on. Is that where we're going?'

'Aye,' she muttered bad-temperedly. 'The Pine Lodge. But don't ask me what the food is like. I've never been in the place. It's near the river and it's always full of lawyers and bank managers from Inverness up for a day's salmon fishing.'

He put the map away and said casually, 'If it's half decent we can spend the rest of the day exploring the area then book a room for the night.'

Her hand tightened on the wheel and she let the car coast to the next passing place where she pulled in and stopped. Staring stonily ahead through the windscreen, she said quietly, 'You can book two rooms if you want to stay, but not one.'

He turned in his seat and sighed. 'I wish you

wouldn't make things difficult, Catriona. I thought we had an agreement.'

'The only thing I agreed to do was to show you around the country,' she reminded him coldly.

He frowned for a moment, then his face cleared. 'You're right! I remember now. I said we'd discuss your other obligations later, didn't I?' His hand reached up and he stroked her hair. 'Well, now is as good a time as any to establish the ground rules.'

She pushed his hand away angrily. 'Stop doing that. I don't like you touching me.'

'Then why are you suddenly so breathless?' he said softly in her ear. 'And why are you so flushed?' His cool fingers brushed the tender skin of her neck. 'You're burning up. Some sort of fever, is it?'

Her throat was closing up, and she swallowed and said unevenly, 'No, damn you. It's anger, if you must know.'

'It looks more like desire to me. The classic symptoms of a woman on the edge of arousal.' His voice was a low, seductive whisper now, and no matter how much she tried to ignore it his words made her tremble. 'Why don't you do the sensible thing? Let's both forget the past. Forget about all the stories you may have heard about me, and I'll forget about Trixie Trotter.'

He watched her closely and saw her lower lip quiver slightly. 'Look...' he went on gently. 'Let's pretend we've just met. We'll make a new start and—'

She whirled on him and poured scorn over the idea. 'I'd rather pretend that we'd never met in the first place. Meeting you was the worst thing that ever happened to me. The second worst was having you follow me here.'

Well, she certainly wasn't backward in making her feelings clear, he thought. He liked that. It was a refreshing change to meet someone with real character, and, in his view, that was an even more attractive quality than stunning good looks. As he looked down into her clear blue eyes he felt an unaccustomed warmth in his heart and he wondered...

He'd gone down that road once with a girl he'd met at university and it had only led to pain and disillusionment. Something was telling him that this time it could be different.

He was stroking her hair again, and it was all she could do not to shake like a leaf as his fingers brushed lightly against her neck. With a scowl of exasperation she broke free and switched on the ignition.

For the next couple of miles there was blessed silence, giving her blood pressure time to get back to normal, then he asked suddenly, 'Who is this woman called Madge your mother was telling me about? Is she a good friend of yours?'

'I work for her,' she replied calmly. 'She owns a fashionable boutique in the King's Road. She gave me a job and a place to live.'

'So she's the one who owns the flat at Palmerston Court?'

'That's right. Now just be quiet and let me concentrate on the driving.'

'You're doing just fine,' he growled. 'So tell me about this woman. And this time tell me the truth. I don't want any more of your lies.'

She took her eyes off the road for a moment and gave him a look of sizzling anger. '*My* lies!' she exploded. 'You've got the bloody nerve to sit there and accuse *me* of lying?' She looked at the road again in time to slow down for a couple of hill sheep ambling along the verge. 'You were the one who did all the lying,' she said bitterly. 'You probably don't realise you're doing it. It's just second nature to a cheat like you.'

He remained unmoved, and when her tirade was over he remarked thoughtfully, 'That idea of dressing up as Trixie Trotter and making sure there was a photographer on hand at the next table…that must have taken a lot of planning. You must have needed a hand to organise it and my guess is that it was your friend Madge. In fact maybe the whole thing was her idea. Am I right?'

Her knuckles tightened on the wheel. If she denied it then she'd be guilty as in his accusation, of lying, so she muttered, 'What if she was?'

'Then I'd say that she was being a bad influence on a foolish and impressionable—'

'You're right there,' she snapped. 'I *was* foolish and impressionable, but the only bad influence I ever met was you. My biggest regret is that Madge wasn't there at the time to warn me about you. She knew all about your reputation as a…a womaniser.'

'Did she now?' he mused aloud. 'And what else does she know?'

'She knows that you got thrown out of the Army,' she answered spitefully.

'I resigned my commission,' he corrected.

'Just so that you wouldn't be court-martialled for disobeying orders. It's the same thing, isn't it?' she said with disdain.

He let the question go and gave a sour laugh. 'She

seems to be remarkably well informed. Or an interfering old gossip, if you look at it another way.'

She wasn't standing for that, and she defended Madge stoutly. 'Just you watch your mouth. You're not fit to speak her name. She might have her faults but at least she's genuine, which is more than anyone can say about you.'

He grinned and raised his hands in a gesture of surrender. 'OK! I give in. I believe you. I won't mention her name again.'

She relaxed once more and they drove the next few miles in silence. In spite of the air-conditioning she lowered the side window and felt the cool breeze tugging at her hair. From the occasional glances she stole at him she could see that he was busy making notes and comparing the landscape with the map which was spread out on his knee. Whatever he was doing he seemed to be going about it in a professional manner. But then, she got the impression that he was a man who never did anything by half measures. Especially when it came to seducing women, she added mentally. He really put all his energy into that. But why? Other people fell in love. Why not him? Was there something driving him to act the way he did?

For an instant their eyes met as he caught her looking at him, and she fixed her eyes hurriedly back on the road. Her thin skirt had ridden too far up her thighs and she wriggled in her seat and pulled at the hem until it was demurely just above her knees.

They'd soon be at the hotel and her heart began to beat just that little bit faster. What was she going to do if he went ahead and booked only one room? Should she just give in, telling herself that she was doing it against her will because of his threat? But

that wouldn't be the truth, would it? The truth was
that there was something stirring…something beginning to send little signals throughout her body.
Something which had a memory of a night in London
and was demanding to be refreshed.

She tried to ignore it but it wouldn't leave, and at
every turn of the wheel it became stronger and more
urgent. It must be the heat, she decided. She'd give
anything for a long, cool dip in a river. Anything to
stop her fevered imagination tormenting her like this.
She concentrated furiously on the road ahead, but the
ghost of his reflection was on the windscreen.

Supposing she did agree to spend the night with
him, as he was demanding. That was all he wanted,
wasn't it? When it was over he'd lose all interest in
her as he'd done before and find someone else. After
that he'd be someone else's problem. But could she
live with herself afterwards, knowing that she'd given
in willingly because of her own weakness? Worst of
all would be the knowledge that he had won in the
end and that all her promises and plans for revenge
had come to nothing. She would just become another
one of his victims, used not once but twice, and then
discarded while he sailed off triumphantly into the
sunset with another colour nailed to his mast.

The fact that she was even contemplating allowing
him to have his way with her again filled her with
contempt for her lack of character and self-discipline.
Surely no man, no matter how sexually attractive he
might be, should have that effect on a woman? If she
was sensible she had to keep in mind that there was
more to a relationship than that. What about true
love…and compassion…and self-sacrifice? Those

were the things that really mattered in the end, weren't they?

He glanced at the dashboard to check the mileage, then grunted, 'We should be there in ten minutes. Let's hope they've got something decent on the menu. Are you hungry, Catriona?'

'Not particularly,' she murmured, keeping her eye on the road. She should have been, but in the last few minutes her thoughts had found something more important to worry about than the mundane matter of food.

He grinned at her, and her hands tightened nervously on the wheel as he declared, 'I'm ravenous. I'm looking forward to something really tasty.'

CHAPTER SEVEN

THE Pine Lodge was one of those grand, early Victorian houses built as a summer retreat for some long-forgotten captain of industry from the English Midlands. Although the interior had undergone a thorough modernisation, the exterior, with its arched windows and long, flagged terrace, still bore witness to a gentler age of elegance and style. It lay between the road and the broad, fast-flowing river to the rear.

Catriona swung the car into the car park and came to rest between a Range Rover and a Volvo estate, then took the keys from the ignition and passed them to Ryan. It was a silent and symbolic gesture meant to show that for the moment at least her job was finished and that he had no further call on her services. Whether he'd pay any attention was another matter, of course.

They'd both undid their seat belts, and she was on the point of opening her door when she paused and said quietly, 'Look…I didn't bring a bag with me and my hair is a mess. I don't suppose you've got a comb I could borrow, have you?'

He studied her without criticism, then said, 'You should have kept your window shut. I see what you mean. Well, we can't have you going in to lunch looking like a gypsy wench after a fight with a gamekeeper.' He lifted his jacket from the rear seat and searched in the inside pocket. 'Here you are. Try this.'

If there was one thing she was fussy about it was

using someone else's towel or comb, and she peered at it suspiciously. Thankfully, but not surprisingly, it was faultlessly clean. With muttered thanks she began untangling her long red tresses. When she'd finished she handed the comb back and said, 'If I'd known we were going to stop for lunch at a place like this I'd have worn something decent.'

Again his eyes travelled over her in that provocative way they had. The way that brought her out in a rash and hot flushes. 'You look perfectly charming to me,' he said with straight-faced sincerity. 'A picture of young, unsullied innocence, as the Reverend McPhee might say.'

There was a stinging reply she could have made to that, but she let it go and followed him in tight-lipped silence towards the entrance. She badly needed a drink. Something in a tall, frosted glass with lots of ice, which would take away the sticky dryness in her mouth.

They crossed the car park and went into the hotel. While he made enquiries at the reception desk she looked around the main foyer. There was a boutique and the inevitable souvenir shop, and another devoted entirely to fishing tackle. Above a huge open fireplace—thankfully unlit at this time of the year—a salmon the size of a baby shark was stuffed and mounted in a glass case. There was a brass plate saying that the fish had been caught in 1960 in the river to the rear. There was nothing like giving your customers a bit of inspiration and motivation for staying another few days, she thought wryly.

She watched Ryan chatting with the pretty blonde receptionist, who seemed to be having trouble looking cool and efficient and kept wetting her cupid's bow

lips with the tip of a pink tongue. Poor fool, she
thought. If only she knew who she was trying to impress. The Lothario of London...Jack the Stripper.
She wouldn't be fluttering her eyelashes at him then.

Finally he came over with a satisfied look on his
face. 'The place is only half full so there's no trouble
with accommodation. The dining room won't be open
again until dinner this evening, but they serve bar
lunches in the lounge.'

At the mention of the word 'accommodation' she
should have put her foot down, but she hadn't, and
now she found herself staring at him, tongue-tied with
indecision. The matter was taken out of her hands
when he gripped her arm and led her towards the
lounge. She swallowed nervously. It wasn't too late.
He hadn't gone ahead and booked a room yet. She
would find a chance some time during the meal to
refuse and make her feelings clear to him. But time
was getting short.

They found a table at a window overlooking the
river and a waiter instantly appeared. Ryan ordered a
whisky and soda for himself and a chilled lemon and
lime for her, then they both consulted the menu.

'I think I'll try the venison steak,' he said. 'It
should be good in this part of the country.'

She chose a ploughman's lunch without the cucum-
ber, then tried to compose herself as the waiter hurried
away. Glancing around the room, she saw that most
of the customers were middle-aged men of the hunting and fishing type. The few women she could see
were dressed in tweed suits and sensible brogues. A
boring but thoroughly respectable lot. They'd have
raised their hands in horror if they only knew what

was going on at this table, she thought. Blackmail, sex and scandal, no less.

When the drinks came she took a hurried gulp at hers. The chill pained her temples but it also brought inspiration, and she smiled at him innocently. 'You won't find any hotels up here who'll take guests who arrive without luggage of some sort.'

'Even if they pay in advance?' he asked, equally innocently.

She gave a self-righteous frown. 'Especially if they offer to pay in advance. Unlike the hotels you frequent in London, they're very old fashioned about "that" type of guest. More so if he's in female company.' She looked down at her left hand and said dryly, 'Surely it must be quite obvious to everyone that we aren't married.'

For a moment his brow furrowed at this obstacle to his plans, then it cleared and he said briskly, 'Then it's lucky for us that I still have a large suitcase in the boot of the car. It's only full of my clean shirts and socks and underwear, but I doubt if they'll go to the lengths of looking inside. And neither will they be looking for a wedding ring. Hotel staff hate to embarrass their guests by asking awkward questions. Anyway, if you don't go around flaunting your left hand no one will be any the wiser.'

She scowled back at his mocking grey eyes. 'And what am I supposed to wear?' she demanded. 'I have nothing but what you see me in. I haven't even got a comb, for heaven's sake!'

'I'm sure the hotel can provide anything you need. There are shops in the foyer, aren't there? When we've booked in you can pick up anything you require and put it on the bill.' He sipped at his whisky and suddenly his voice became softly threatening. 'You're trying desperately to think up every obstacle you can to prevent the inevitable, but it won't work and you're beginning to try my patience again.' He withdrew the car keys from his pocket and laid them on the table. 'You can make your choice now, Catriona. Either you agree to spend the night here with me or you can drive me back to Kindarroch as soon as we've had lunch. When we get there I'll pick up the rest of my belongings and get out of your life for ever—but not before I've nailed up copies of that picture in the hotel bar, the post office, and on the church noticeboard.'

Looking into those hard eyes, she knew it wasn't merely a threat. It was an ultimatum. For an instant her hands clenched, then the anger seemed to leave her, only to be replaced by a curious feeling of relief. Now she could honestly say that she'd tried her best. Whatever happened now, at least her conscience was clear.

'All right,' she said in tired surrender. 'You've got me exactly where you want me. I'll not have you break my parents' hearts. But everyone has a conscience, Ryan. Even you. I just hope that some day it'll come back to haunt you as you deserve.'

He treated her to a thin, sardonic smile. 'I doubt that very much. In years to come I'm sure I'll have fond memories of this night.' He raised his glass in a mock toast. 'Here's to sweet revenge. You must have thought much the same when you made a fool of me in Cardini's.'

There wasn't much she could say to that, so she shifted uncomfortably in her seat and studiously avoided looking at him.

When the meal came she picked away daintily at

hers, trying to drag it out as long as possible. On the other hand he had cleared his plate ten minutes ago, and now he sat watching her in amused silence as she chased the last pickled onion around the plate with her fork. Suddenly he reached over, grabbed the pickle between his finger and thumb and held it to her mouth. Their eyes met and held, and finally she parted her lips and accepted it.

He grinned at her and remarked casually, 'There are some men who are put off kissing by the smell of onions on a girl's breath. Speaking from experience, it's never bothered me. I guess you're lucky.'

'Am I?' she asked dryly. 'Perhaps I should have asked for garlic.'

He gave a taunting smile. 'That's for protection against vampires. But don't worry. I won't bite your neck during the night. I'm not giving guarantees about any other part of your body, however.'

She flushed, and hissed at him over the table, 'Stop saying things like that! It…it's…' She tried to think of a word but he cut in.

'It's getting you all flustered? Yes, I can see that.' He grinned. 'Well, just pretend that you're Trixie Trotter for the night. She wouldn't be the least bit embarrassed, would she?'

She wondered if it wouldn't be wiser just to keep her stupid mouth shut. Every time she spoke she was just providing him with more ammunition to fire.

They left the bar and returned to the foyer. Gesturing towards the shops, he said, 'Have a look around and pick out anything you need. I'll get the case from the car and sign us in.'

He strode off and left her as if the whole thing was cut and dried. For a moment she just stared after him helplessly, then, reminding herself that she had already made the decision and that it was cut and dried after all, she composed herself with a deep breath and made her way over to the shops.

In the first shop she bought a comb, a toothbrush and toothpaste, and various other toiletries which took her fancy. But it was in the boutique where the real spending began. After all, *he* was paying, and if he wanted her to act like Trixie Trotter she'd go ahead and spend like Trixie Trotter.

By the time Ryan returned and found her she was waiting, feeling a little smug and pleased with herself, while the salesgirl wrapped up her purchases.

'Have you got everything you need, darling?' he asked pleasantly, casting a benevolent eye over the clutch of carrier bags on the counter.

She returned his smile. 'Yes, dear. I think so. But if I've forgotten anything I can always get them to send it up, can't I?'

'Of course you can, sweetheart.'

She took the hastily made up invoice from the flustered and envious salesgirl and handed it to him with an innocent smile. 'You'll see to this, will you, dear?'

'Certainly, my precious.' Barely glancing at it, he pulled out his chequebook and remarked humorously, 'I'm glad to see the treatment is working at last.' Then he leaned over the counter and said to the salesgirl in a confidential whisper which could be heard a hundred yards away, 'She used to be a terrible shopaholic. A really hopeless case. The result of a deprived childhood. I could never let her out on her own.'

Catriona gave him an icy look, then grabbed the carrier bags and marched back into the foyer. The porter took them up in the lift and showed them to the room, where Ryan gave him a generous tip then firmly closed the door.

The room was comfortably furnished and carpeted and provided a magnificent view back down the glen. She examined the bathroom carefully and found it pristine and shining. Standing on tiptoe, she ran a finger along the top of the strip lighting over the sink. Back in the main room she did the same thing to the windowledges and chair-backs.

When she'd finished her inspection he said dryly, 'How about the top of the picture rail? I'll lift you up if you like.'

'I hate slovenly housekeeping,' she told him calmly. 'If you've spent most of your time living in hotels you're probably used to it, but I'm particular where I sleep.' She marched over to the bed...it would be a four poster, wouldn't it?...and pulled back the duvet. The sheets looked crisp and snowy white.

'Well...?' he queried. 'Good enough for you? Or would you rather we tried it out first before making up your mind?'

Ignoring that remark, she took one final look around the room, then said, 'I'm going to shower and change. I suggest you make yourself scarce for half an hour or so. Go down to the bar or take a walk outside.'

He remained where he was, so she repeated herself sharply, adding, 'Go on, then! Don't just stand there.'

You had to admire her style, he thought. And, looking at that determined little mouth and the imperious tilt of the head, he was more determined than ever to bite through that hot, peppery crust and get to the soft and utterly feminine creature below.

'There's no hurry,' he said easily. 'I reckon this is

as good a time as any to sit down for a while and talk things over.'

He was quite prepared for the raw suspicion in her eyes when she demanded, 'What things?'

'This and that,' he offered with a nonchalant shrug and an open smile meant to put her at her ease. 'We can surely exchange points of view like two civilised people, can't we?'

'I already know what your point of view is,' she said tartly. 'Regarding women, in particular. And it certainly isn't civilised.'

He could see he was going to have his work cut out here, but in all fairness he supposed he couldn't blame her—even though she had been a major contributor to her own predicament. He'd tried earlier on to put the record straight but she hadn't given him a chance. She was an impulsive little fire-brand who believed in shooting from the lip. Still, there was no harm in trying again.

'Look...' he said patiently. 'Don't be such a bad-tempered little...' He stopped, realising by the way she bristled that he'd pressed the wrong button again, and he listened in exasperation to her outburst.

'Is it any wonder I'm bad-tempered?' she demanded hotly. 'First of all you...and then you...'

He only half listened to her tirade, in which she likened him to everyone from Caligula to Vlad the Impaler, and watched her in fascination. She really was a sight to behold, he thought. She had.... Chutzpah! That was the word. Why the hell hadn't he met someone like her years ago?

She was still putting him through the shredder, and he grinned as she slowly ran out of steam. '...means nothing to you,' she said breathlessly. 'There's only one thing on your mind. You know it and I know it. First it's threats of blackmail…now you want me to sit down and listen to more of your lies, hoping that I'll be stupid enough to…to…' She drew a deep breath, then pointed a quivering finger at the door. 'Now please go and allow me to have my shower.'

He grinned again. There was more than one way to skin a cat—or to prove a point to someone who was too stubborn to listen. Miss Catriona McNeil needed her claws trimmed a little.

He slowly removed his jacket, then loosened his tie.

'What do you think you're doing?' she asked, eyeing him uncertainly.

He was unbuttoning his shirt now. 'Getting undressed, of course. We may as well shower together.'

Her eyes widened in trepidation. 'Shower *together*!' She gulped. 'Certainly not! 'It…it's…'

She'd been going to say 'indecent,' but he butted in. 'It's practical. We can sponge each other's backs.'

He advanced on her slowly, then laid his hands gently on her shoulders and looked down deeply into her eyes. 'I'm sure you'll enjoy the experience,'

His lips were close. Far too close. And her legs were getting weak. Damn him! In a voice that was barely above a squeaky whisper, she said, 'The…the shower isn't big enough for both of us. Any fool can see that.'

'Which will make it all the more intimate,' he said with hoarse-sounding relish. His fingers were now slowly and deliberately unbuttoning the front of her blouse, and when it was opened he reached behind and deftly unhooked her bra. She barely had time to gasp before he crushed his lips down onto hers, and then she felt his warm hand cupping and weighing her breast. Her body quivered under the intimate and sexually arousing touch of his hand and she collapsed against him.

'That's much better,' he murmured, taking his mouth from hers and looking down at her with smoky grey eyes. He began caressing the nipple which had burgeoned at the first contact and his lips stretched in a knowing smile. 'The tongue may lie, Catriona, but the body can't. It's aching for love, isn't it? There's only one way to satisfy the longing we both have for each other.'

She looked at him in desperate, heart-thudding silence. Somewhere in the dark and chaotic depths of her mind the cold, clear voice of reason was warning her that if she gave in without a struggle she would never, ever be able to face herself in the mirror again without a feeling of sickening failure and self-contempt. Was that worth a few minutes' pleasure? She was no nearer the answer now than she'd been an hour ago, but now the temptation was becoming more than she could bear.

'Lost your tongue for once?' he asked in a harsh whisper. 'Yet I notice that you can't even bring yourself to deny the truth with a mere shake of the head.' Her skirt landed round her ankles in a heap as he undid the zip, and her heart thumped frantically in her ears as he began kissing her on the neck.

Her hands, which up till now had been hanging helplessly by her sides now made a feeble attempt to push him away but ended up assuming a life of their own and sneaking round to encircle his waist. Feeling the warmth and firmness of his flesh beneath the thin cotton shirt, she couldn't help herself, and her fingertips played over the rippling sinews and muscles of his back.

Sensing her imminent surrender, he gave a growl of pleasure from the depths of his throat and gently slid her briefs down over her hips, leaving her to finish the job by stepping out of them and kicking them aside. The warning voice in her head had gone now, only to be replaced by an exhilarating feeling of unrestrained wantonness. He was a liar, a cheat and a womaniser, and God knows what else besides, but she didn't give a damn. Her heart was pounding and the rush of blood was singing in her ears. She wanted him. She wanted him now.

After all her good intentions and protestations she was no better than one of those foolish women Madge had warned her about—the type who were attracted by unscrupulous devils like him.

But she didn't care. This aching desire was more than anyone could bear. She sought his lips greedily as she thrust herself harder against him and trembled with ecstasy as he stroked and firmly pressed the taut, firm flesh of her buttocks.

Their kisses were filled with a fiery, hungry passion for each other and her fingers scrabbled feverishly at his trouser belt.

'You want me, don't you, Catriona?' he asked huskily. 'I want to hear you say it.'

Was he mad? Of course she wanted him! Couldn't he tell, for God's sake! 'Yes…yes, Ryan. I do,' she moaned, her voice bubbling in her throat.

'Good…' he said. 'Then I can't be accused of forcing myself on you, can I? You're as willing to make love with me now as you were on that first night.'

There was something in his voice that made her

blink the haze of hot desire away from her eyes, and she stared in incomprehension at the taunting smile on his face.

'You're quite right, of course,' he drawled. 'The shower cubicle is far too small and cramped for such an activity. You might slip on the soap and break a leg. On the grounds of safety alone I think it would be wiser to wait until tonight. The bed looks more than adequate for our purposes.'

The words hit her like a deluge of icy water and she made a vain effort to cover her modesty as the full horror of the truth sank in. For a moment her mouth worked in silent outrage then she managed a muffled screech. 'You...you pig! You rotten... unfeeling bastard! I...I'll...'

He stifled her outburst with a kiss, then he whirled her round and gave her a gentle smack on the bare bottom. 'That's not the kind of language a lady should use. Now go and have your shower. I'll be back in half an hour.' With that he pushed her in the direction of the shower, then left the room.

As the door closed behind him she glared at it in outrage, then beat her clenched fist against her forehead. He was a scheming...manipulative...monster. He'd laid a trap to expose the shallowness of her pretence, and oh, how easily she'd fallen in to it. If it had been a deliberate attempt to destroy her self-confidence and make her want to curl up and die he'd succeeded.

The shower cleaned her and cooled her down, and her anger at him was put on the back boiler as she dressed herself. She had carefully removed the labels from the new underwear and she had got as far as donning briefs and bra when he opened the door and came sauntering back in.

He stopped to blatantly admire her. 'Pure silk? Very sexy-looking, Catriona. It's a pity you have to wear anything on top. You'd create as big a sensation in the dining room here, as you did at Cardini's.'

She studiously ignored him and eased herself into a pair of pale green cotton trousers, but she couldn't ignore him for long. From the corner of her eye she saw him begin to undress. First came the shoes, then socks and shirt. And then the trousers, which he carefully folded across the back of a chair.

It was the nonchalant and unconcerned way he went about it that worried her. Either the man was completely shameless or he was deliberately demonstrating his lack of respect for her feelings. When he at last casually removed his briefs she reddened as he caught her staring at him, and she hurriedly turned her back on him and slid into a blouse, only to hear him chuckling to himself as he made for the shower.

She was staring out of the window grimly, her arms folded and her foot tapping, when he emerged five minutes later. From his reflection in the window she saw that he'd at least had the decency to drape himself in a towel this time.

She had her eyes fixed on a fisherman who was trying a long cast to the far side of the river when Ryan said, 'You can turn round now and stop blushing. I'm decent.'

With a disdainful sniff she turned from the window, prepared to give him the sharp edge of her tongue, but she blinked in surprise and tried to stifle a laugh at the sight of him in his boxer shorts.

'I see you recognise them.' He grinned. 'Bright red

with little yellow teddy bears. They're the ones you dropped in my lap in Cardini's. Not my style, really, but I thought I'd keep them as a memento.'

'You said you were decent,' she muttered crossly. 'Put your damn trousers on.'

Enjoying her discomfort, he hummed under his breath as he began dressing, and with a haughty look she marched past him towards the door and said stiffly, 'I'll wait for you down in the foyer.'

Downstairs she settled herself on one of the comfortable settees, picked a magazine at random from the table and idly flicked through the pages. Unable to get interested in it, she put it back on the table, then her eye was caught by the public telephone at the side of the reception desk and she wondered if she should call her mother and warn her that she wouldn't be home tonight. But what reason could she give? She couldn't very well tell her the truth or the whole McNeil clan would rush here to her rescue and the fat would really be in the fire. She'd have to make up some plausible story for the sake of everyone's peace of mind.

Damn the man for causing her all this grief and hassle. And how many other lives had he screwed up in his relentless pursuit of selfish pleasure? Did he ever stop to wonder about that? No, of course he didn't. He just sailed on, oblivious to the cries of distress and broken hearts in his wake.

She was still smarting from the humiliation he'd caused her over the shower. And in more ways than one, she thought bitterly. It didn't do a lot for a girl's self-respect when a man could turn down such a blatant offer as she'd given him, only to be told that he'd take her up on it later on. It was embarrassing to say the least.

It left her with the feeling that either the man had iron self-control or else sex was nothing more than a game to him. A game to be played entirely at his convenience and it was just her hard luck to be one of the pawns.

She'd been staring at her feet gloomily, and happened to look up just as he came striding towards her.

He stopped and ran an approving eye over her as she rose, but before he could say anything she held her hand out. 'You'll have to lend me some coins for the phone. My mother will be worried if I don't return home tonight.'

He dug in his pocket, then offered innocently, 'Would you like me to explain the situation to her?'

She grabbed the coins from his hand and snapped, 'No, I wouldn't.' Leaving him standing there, she marched over to the phone, her brain already concocting a plausible story about the car breaking down in Inverness and no spares being available until tomorrow.

When that unpleasant job was over she replaced the phone and found him waiting for her outside on the terrace. 'All right...' she said coolly, surveying the scenery. 'So what are we going to do now? Spend an exciting afternoon looking at the river?'

He handed her the keys to the car again and gave his orders. 'I want to see as much of the area around here as possible, and you are going to do the driving.'

Shrugging indifferently, she followed him down into the car park. She would dearly have loved to know what he found so interesting in a wild and remote place like this, but she'd have sooner bitten off her tongue than ask. If he wanted to waste his time she wasn't going to stop him. At least he'd be sensible enough not to toy with her emotions while she was driving.

Taking her directions from him, she turned right onto a particularly narrow road about a mile past the hotel. Slowing to little more than walking pace, to avoid the worst holes in the neglected road surface, she complained to him, 'Are you sure about this? I don't think this road goes anywhere. It looks abandoned.'

Hardly looking up from the map he was consulting, he growled at her again. 'Keep driving. I'll tell you when to stop.'

Bad-mannered lout, she thought. It would serve him right if they ended up with broken suspension or a buckled wheel.

There was nothing to be seen except for the occasional white-painted croft nestling in the heather and bracken at the foot of a mountain, where some poor family kept body and soul together with the aid of a milk cow, a few sheep and chickens and a few acres of cultivated ground.

They were near one of such crofts when he told her to stop the car so they could get out and stretch their legs. She looked around her and said quietly, 'It's not much like the King's Road on a Saturday afternoon, is it? I told you that I don't think this road leads anywhere. We'd be as well turning back.'

He was breathing deeply at the air, and his grey eyes were narrowly scanning and studying the lie of the land, when he said quietly, 'Someone's watching us.'

She blinked and glanced around. 'Who? I don't see anyone.'

'That's because whoever it is is taking great care to conceal himself in the heather.'

She looked around her again, then eyed him in disbelief. 'There's no one here except us. You're just trying to scare me, aren't you?'

'He's the one who's scared,' he declared softly. 'That's why he's hiding. It's probably a poacher and he thinks we represent authority.' He took her hand and grinned. 'Let's go and have a chat with him.'

She allowed herself to be led up the side of a narrow peat-coloured burn for about a hundred yards and then she saw the figure of a small boy crouching down in the undergrowth, only his dirt-streaked face and a mop of dark curly hair visible. He stood up as they approached—all five feet of him—and eyed them warily, ready to take instant flight.

Ryan grinned and picked up the home-made fishing rod which was lying at the boy's feet. 'Having any luck, son?'

The boy looked at each of them in turn before deciding that they were no threat, then he shook his head.

Ryan glanced down into the slow-moving stream. 'There should be plenty of trout in there. What are you using? Worms?'

The boy nodded. 'Aye.' He wiped his nose with the back of his hand, then shrugged. 'There's nothing else to use, is there?'

Catriona smiled at the boy. He probably came from the croft which lay about half a mile away. There were carefully patched holes in his jeans and his ragged shirt had seen better days.

'You don't need worms to catch trout, son,' Ryan said with a quiet smile. 'All you need is one hand. Hasn't your father showed you that trick?'

The boy shook his head and muttered, 'My dad was killed. He was a soldier.'

Ryan stared down at him in silence for a moment, then he ruffled the mop of dark hair and said quietly, 'I could show you how, if you want to learn.'

The boy nodded eagerly and Ryan grinned. 'OK. Let's look for a good spot.'

They walked quietly upstream until Ryan suddenly looked at both of them, silencing them with a finger pressed to his lips. Removing his shirt, he lay down at right angles to the stream and lowered his hand gently until it was lying palm upwards on the bottom. She and the boy both crouched down and saw the large brown speckled trout swimming gently upstream. When it was directly over Ryan's palm he moved his fingers, lightly stroking the fish's belly. The trout, obviously enjoying this new sensation, remained where it was. Ryan continued stroking for another few seconds, then he jerked his arm upwards and the fish went sailing over their heads to land behind them.

The boy gave a yelp of delight and Ryan stood up. 'See how easy it is, son? Now we'll move to another spot and then you can try. Just remember not to grab the fish or you'll lose it like a bar of wet soap. Just scoop it out quickly.'

It was an hour later when they returned to the car, and Ryan grinned at Catriona and nodded towards the distant croft. 'Well, that's one family who'll be having a decent meal of grilled trout this evening.'

There was nothing boastful in the way he'd said it.

Just a satisfaction that he'd been able to help someone. She looked at him strangely. She knew she'd never forget the look of adoration on the boy's face as he'd thanked Ryan before skipping off home with his catch of three. She'd almost felt like kissing him herself.

As she resumed driving she said, 'I've seen that done before. It's called guddling. It's a real old poacher's trick. Where did you learn?'

'In the Army. I did survival training about fifty miles south of here. They drop you by helicopter in the middle of the night with nothing but a map, a compass, a knife and a piece of flint. Then they send a hunting party out to look for you. You have to stay free and survive for twenty-one days.' He finished on a note of nostalgia, as if he missed the life and the challenges it had provided.

She chanced another glance at him…at the craggy profile, the strength and determination in the set of the jaw. He was one hundred and ten per cent male. And most of all he was a survivor. And if he was a survivor what did that make her? What chance did little old her have against the likes of him? Well, at least it was going to be interesting finding out.

Knowing that she should really be giving him the coldest shoulder possible, she was nevertheless becoming intrigued enough to ask him suddenly, 'If you liked the Army so much why did you refuse to obey orders?'

She'd expected and was prepared for a verbal rap over the knuckles, to be told to mind her own damn business, but to her surprise he seemed quite willing to talk about it.

'It was during one of those civil wars in Southern

Europe,' he replied with some bitterness. 'Neighbours were killing neighbours in the name of religion. The UN had organised a ceasefire but the rebels kept firing from their side on a village next to our camp. They'd killed hundreds with their indiscriminate shelling. My men and I wanted to wipe the gun position out but we were under strict orders not to cross the border.' He paused for a moment and she saw him pass a tired hand over his brow before continuing. 'When a shell landed on the local infant school it was more than I or my men could stand. We told the UN observer to go to hell, we crossed the border and destroyed the gun emplacement.'

She brought the car slowly to a halt then turned in her seat and stared at him. 'And they made you resign because of that?' she asked in a voice of quiet outrage.

He shrugged. 'Someone had to be sacrificed to appease the politicians.'

Her mouth worked in silence for a moment, then she said forthrightly, 'The bloody idiots! I'd have given you a medal.'

He turned those steady grey eyes on her, then asked, 'Why?'

'Because I'd have done exactly the same as you if I'd been a soldier,' she said bluntly.

The eyes continued to study her, then he nodded and smiled broadly. 'I guess you would have, Catriona. Whether you like it or not, you and I are alike in many ways, aren't we?'

She had a sudden feeling that she was getting into dangerous ground here, and she looked away uncomfortably. 'Oh…I doubt that.'

He raised his hand and grabbed her hair, and gave her a long, hard, nerve-tingling kiss. Then he let her go and challenged her harshly, 'You're a girl who is prepared to go to any lengths to seek revenge or rectify a wrong. Well, so will I. There can only be one winner in our little contest, Catriona. The only question that remains is this. How are you going to reconcile yourself to defeat?'

She gulped painfully and gave the only answer she could think of. 'I...I don't know, Ryan. I suppose it depends on how charitable you are in victory.'

The smile on his lips was provocative, and the look in those grey eyes was playing havoc with her already disturbed emotions. Her heartbeat was quickening and pounding in her chest when he asked softly, 'How charitable would you like me to be? Should I just take my pound of flesh and be content with that?'

She struggled to bring the words from the dryness of her mouth. 'Just...just leave me with some self-respect. Th—that's all I ask, Ryan. Destroy those pictures of me so that no one up here will ever know the truth. Give me a chance to make a respectable life for myself after you've gone.'

His dark brows rose a fraction but his eyes held her remorselessly. 'Is that all? I'm disappointed, Catriona. I thought you'd have set your sights higher than that. After all, you are in love with me, aren't you?'

The question stunned her. Not simply because of its directness but because it forced her into sudden confrontation with the very thing she'd been trying to avoid. Up until the last hour or so it had been easy enough to explain her feelings for him as nothing but the result of raw, sexual attraction, because he certainly had nothing else going for him—unless you were stupid enough to think that wealth and power counted for anything. But now she had seen a different side to him. She had seen a man with a generosity of spirit and enough humanity to throw away a career rather than put up with injustice and barbarism.

His eyes still held hers, searching and probing deep into her very soul and still awaiting an answer. With a tremendous effort she managed to rip her gaze away and she stared blindly through the windscreen. Finding her voice at last, she said stiffly, 'Any woman would be a fool to fall in love with you, Ryan. She could never trust you to be faithful, could she? By your own admission you're a man who prefers casual relationships. "On a regular basis" was the phrase you used. I remember it quite clearly. Your idea of being in love is different from mine. It's only the physical pleasure you're obsessed with. Nothing else matters to you.'

Ryan was suddenly filled with a sense of frustration. That had been her conception of him which he'd gone to such lengths to destroy. But apparently it had been a waste of time. No doubt she'd rationalised his behaviour to fit in with her own image of him.

There was one consoling thought however. Instead of outright denial that she was, in spite of everything, still in love with him she'd neatly evaded the question. All she'd said was that a woman would be foolish to fall for an unfaithful hound like him. Was she beginning to crack? He'd find out soon enough, when he judged the time and place to be right. The one thing he was certain of was that he wasn't going to lose her. Now that he'd finally found this wonderful woman he wasn't going to let Catriona McNeil get away again—whatever it took.

CHAPTER EIGHT

THEY'D no sooner settled themselves in a quiet corner of the cocktail lounge than the smartly dressed waiter was by their side with his order book at the ready. Ryan ordered a couple of drinks, then asked for the menu to be sent through.

The soft music and discreet lighting was no doubt designed to promote a feeling of relaxation and well-being, but it was wasted on her. She still felt as edgy and nervous as a candle-flame. Ryan, on the other hand, wore his usual air of relaxed confidence, and the way he kept looking at her with that expression of smouldering relish for things to come did nothing for her peace of mind. He might have won the game, and his night of passion might be assured, but did he have to look so damned pleased with himself about it?

When the drinks and the menu arrived he grinned at her. 'Glenlivet and spring water. That was your favourite, as I recall. Or was that, like everything else, simply said in order to impress me?'

'I've no idea what you're talking about,' she muttered self-consciously.

'Liar.'

'Don't you dare call me a liar!' she snapped.

He raised a thin dark eyebrow at her in surprise. 'Why not? That's exactly what you are.' His grey eyes, half angry and half amused, invited her to reply defiantly but she merely glared at him in silence and he finally sighed and opened the menu with a flourish. 'It doesn't matter. Now, what would you like to eat? How about the poached salmon? I should think that any chef in this part of the country can do culinary marvels with freshly caught salmon.'

'I'm not really that hungry,' she told him, recovering some poise and examining her fingernails. 'My appetite seems to have gone.'

'Drink your apéritif,' he suggested with a tender smile of exaggerated compassion. 'That will bring it back.' Without consulting her further, he signalled the waiter again and gave the order.

'After dinner we'll have a quiet stroll along the riverbank and enjoy the evening air,' he announced cheerfully. 'It's the end of a lovely summer day and the stars will soon be out. It should put you in the mood for romance.'

Romance? she thought bitterly. Was that what he called it? She took a delicate sip of her drink then replaced the glass and looked up slowly to meet his eyes in heated challenge. 'Just how long do you intend staying in Kindarroch?'

He feigned a look of surprise. 'I thought I'd made that clear to you yesterday. This part of the country is ripe for development. All it needs is someone to drag it into the twentieth century.'

'And that someone has to be you, does it?' she asked coldly.

He shrugged. 'Why not? It's what I do best. In any case, it's thanks to you that I'm here in the first place so you've no right complaining.'

'I've got every right in the world to complain,' she retorted. 'If you treated women with more respect instead of as mere playthings to satisfy your lust none of this would have happened.'

'You may be right,' he said indifferently. 'But as for all these women you're so concerned about…well, they got no more than they deserved. Most of them gambled and lost, but none of them complained afterwards. Not until you arrived on the scene.'

She could hardly believe she was hearing this. He made Attila the Hun sound like a saint. Of all the conceited, arrogant… 'Are you saying I deserved to be treated like that?' she demanded furiously.

'Let's just say that at the time I believed you did,' he answered suavely. He raised his glass in a mock toast. 'Anyway, there was no harm done, except to your dignity, so let's drink to your continuing good health.'

She clenched her fists and counted very slowly to ten, then spoke as calmly as she could. 'I think it would be better if I went back to London. I'll leave at the end of the week.'

He thought about that for a moment, then shook his head doubtfully. 'That would be a grave mistake, Catriona. It would wreck my plans. Anyway, look what happened to you the last time you went. You were like a lamb in a den of wolves.'

She couldn't argue with that. Then she thought of Morag and muttered, 'I listened to the wrong advice the last time. This time I won't be so stupid.'

'Everyone says that,' he remarked with casual dismissal. 'But they usually keep making the same mistakes.' He stretched over the table and patted the back of her hand paternally. 'Take my word for it. You'd be much safer staying here with me. Better the devil you know than the one you don't, as the old saying goes.'

She'd never really known the meaning of frustration until now. It wasn't very often she was stuck for words but this was one of the times. You couldn't argue with him. And if you insulted him he just smiled and threw it back in your face. She was beginning to get the uneasy feeling that he was deliberately winding her up. Why? Was he looking for more than her mere physical submission? Was he some kind of sadistic fiend intent on turning her into a nervous wreck?

No! That was a stupid idea. She'd seen the good and caring side of his nature. So it had to be something else.

With an air of distraction she made little circles on the tabletop with her glass, then looked up and frowned at him suspiciously. 'Just what exactly is it that you intend doing up here? You're surely not going to renovate and live in the old Duke's hunting lodge?'

He grinned. 'Why not? Wouldn't I make a good lord of the manor?'

'I'd say it would be too boring for a man like you.' She smiled scornfully. 'Just imagine it. No Cardini's. No supply of pretty young women on tap. You wouldn't last more than a month.'

He grinned again, then sighed. 'You're right. But I wouldn't be staying there. I have other ideas for that place.' He studied his glass for a moment, then became quite serious. 'A few months ago I was approached by a couple of men from my old regiment. Sergeants. Good men. Tough and loyal. They're civilians now but they don't want to let all their special service training go to waste. They had this scheme for setting up an adventure centre. The idea has been tried before and it works. The big multinational companies send their promising young executives there for courses on leadership and self-reliance. The men asked me to go into partnership with them and find a suitable place. That hunting lodge is almost in the middle of one of the largest remaining wildernesses in Europe. It's the perfect location for such an enterprise.'

She wished she could find something wrong with the idea but she couldn't, and she said grudgingly, 'I suppose it might work.'

'I'll make damn sure it works,' he asserted cheerfully. 'And it'll need quite a large staff to keep the place running. Naturally they'd all be recruited from the outlying communities and they'd have to live in.' His grey eyes gazed at her innocently. 'How would you like to be in charge of the catering?'

Ignoring that last remark, she said, 'And what about Kindarroch? Are you really going to buy the hotel?'

'I have a surveyor coming from Inverness to look it over tomorrow. I want to extend it and add another twenty rooms.'

'But why?' she asked, genuinely puzzled. 'It hardly pays its way as it is. Not enough tourists come here in the summer. If it wasn't for the bar takings at the weekends they'd have closed years ago.'

'That's because there is absolutely nothing there to attract anyone. Why should anyone want to visit a small fishing village that went into decline years ago? A few artists, perhaps? Poets looking for solitude? At the rate it's going Kindarroch will be nothing but a memory in twenty years' time.'

He was only saying what everyone in Kindarroch knew but were loath to admit.

'And I suppose you're going to change all that?' she asked with a little smile of irony.

'You don't mind if I give it a try, do you?' he retorted with equal sarcasm.

'Only if you leave old Morag in peace,' she said firmly. 'I saw the way you were looking at her cottage. "The best view in Kindarroch," you said. You can't wait to get your grasping hands on it, can you?'

For a moment he just sat looking at her in silence. No. Not at her. It was as if he was looking through her…beyond… She felt gooseflesh prickling up her arm, then the spell was broken and his eyes became sharply focused on hers. 'Your old friend has nothing to fear from me, Catriona. In fact I'd like to reassure her personally. I'd like you to take me to meet her some time.'

'I'll do that.' And she'd make sure he put any promise he made down in writing, she thought grimly. 'So how exactly do you intend dragging my village into the twentieth century?' she demanded.

'I'm going to turn it into the finest marina north of the Med,' he announced casually. 'Everything is already there. It has one of the safest harbours on the west coast and plenty of room for development. In three years' time you'll never recognise the place.'

She stared at him, then almost shuddered. 'You can't be serious! We've had these weekend sailors with their flashy yachts and motor cruisers before. They come ashore, lording it over everyone. They bring all their fancy food and drink with them, so they never contribute anything to the local economy, and when they've gone they leave the place littered with junk and all the trash they've tossed overboard.' She eyed him with derision. 'The villagers aren't going to thank you for that.'

'I wouldn't expect them to,' he answered patiently. 'But there won't be any weekend sailors to worry about. It's settlers I want to attract. High-powered executives with their families. They'll love the peace and quiet of the Western Highlands. Hunting, shooting, fishing and sailing right on their doorstep.'

She almost laughed aloud. The flaw in the idea was so obvious. 'And how are these "high-powered executives" going to commute to their offices in London? Are you going to build an airstrip as well?' she asked caustically. 'By the time they get home at night it'll be time to put the cat out.'

'They won't have to commute anywhere,' he replied calmly. 'Haven't you heard? This is the age of the information highway. Do you realise that the average executive in London does as much work while stuck in some traffic jam somewhere by using a cell phone and a laptop computer as he does in his office? He can be in instantaneous touch with his secretary in Manchester or his head salesman in Tokyo. The days of the office block are over. They're too expensive and take up too much valuable real estate.' He grinned at her look of wonder. 'In Kindarroch there'll be a business centre with state-of-the-art technology. Everything they could conceivably need will be there. And just think of the jobs it'll bring.'

It took her breath away. Whatever else he might be he was undoubtedly a man with one hell of an imagination. And she hadn't the slightest doubt that he could do it. If he was as ruthless and single-minded in business as he was in the pursuit of women then he was bound to succeed.

'Well, if you pull it off, they'll probably erect a statue to you on the harbour wall,' she said bitterly. 'You'll forgive me if I stay away from the unveiling, won't you?'

That taunting little grin was back on his lips as he remonstrated, 'Come now, Catriona. Don't be such a spoilsport. After all, if there is any credit to be given I insist that you share it with me. If it hadn't been for you I'd never have heard of Kindarroch.'

'Don't remind me,' she muttered.

She remained tense during dinner, only managing to pick away without much enthusiasm at the delicious meal. Thankfully Ryan made no attempt to indulge in small talk, and for that at least she was grateful. It gave her time to ponder her situation. On second thoughts perhaps that was a deliberate ploy on his part. Just let her stew in her own juice. When it came to exacting revenge, the McNeils had nothing to teach him.

She'd never, ever been anything other than ruthlessly honest with herself, and if she applied that to her present situation she was forced to admit that the thought of making love with him tonight made her dry-mouthed with anticipation. She could easily rationalise her guilt away by reminding herself that she was only doing it to save her family from shame. No one needed to tell her that that was a specious argument but it would have to do. Her desire to be possessed by him once more might be primitive but it was also a demon which wasn't going to be ignored and forgotten just because it wasn't welcome.

Her real problem was just over the horizon. If he'd

intended returning to London when he'd got what he'd come for she could have lived with that. He'd have been gone for good and she could have readjusted her life accordingly.

But he wasn't going to leave. From the grandiose plans he'd just unfolded it looked as if he intended taking up permanent residence. And he'd also given broad hints at his displeasure should she decide to leave. What the hell was his idea? Did he think she'd stand for being his personal concubine to be on hand whenever he felt like it?

Instead of having coffee when the meal was over he took her back to the cocktail lounge for another whisky.

'Are you intending to get me drunk?' she demanded quietly when they were seated.

'Perish the thought,' he answered glibly. 'I don't think there's any need for that. The look of resignation on your face as you sat through the meal told me all I want to know.' He bared his teeth in a satyr's grin. 'But I've a deep-down feeling that beneath that sour expression your little heart is beating wildly in anticipation of the pleasures ahead.'

She looked away uncomfortably. 'You're impossible. You're a disgrace to your sex.'

'Perhaps,' he admitted with frankness. 'I'm no angel, but at least I'm honest... Unlike some people I can think of, I've never pretended to be something I'm not.'

It had the unmistakable ring of an accusation and she looked at him sharply. 'I suppose you're going to drag Trixie Trotter back from the dead?'

He returned her look with an even sharper one of his own. 'I wasn't thinking of that misguided escapade, my dear girl. I was remembering the conversation we had when we first met.'

Her face went blank and he continued softly, 'It was only a few weeks ago, Catriona. Surely you haven't forgotten the start of it all and the lies you told me?'

She sat up rigidly, almost bristling with anger, aware but uncaring of the covert glances in her direction. 'That's the third time today you've accused me of lying!' she said in a fury. 'I resent that strongly. Either you apologise right now or I'll...I'll...'

'You'll what?' he asked, raising a darkly mocking eyebrow in challenge.

She sat and glared at him for a moment, then she pushed her chair back, got angrily to her feet and stormed her way to the exit.

He caught up with her in the foyer, and, grabbing her tightly by the arm, he unobtrusively steered her towards the main entrance and out onto the terrace. There he pulled her to a stop and looked down into her flushed and angry face. 'All right. Calm down, you impetuous little fire-eater. I apologise. Instead of saying that you lied to me I should perhaps have said that you misled me. There, does that make you feel any better?'

'No, it bloody well doesn't,' she fumed.

'Then perhaps this will.' With an abruptness which shocked her into startled immobility he yanked her head back and kissed her savagely on the lips.

Recovering her wits, she tried to break away, but her strength was no match for his and she gave up the struggle. Determined not to respond, she kept her body stiff and her lips rigid, but as the assault continued she began to melt in the heat of aroused passion and she could feel her legs going.

At last he released her, looked down into her dazed eyes, and, to her chagrin, remarked cynically, 'You can't decide whether to be consumed by anger or desire, can you? Your red hair should have warned me, but now I know how to deal with your tantrums in future. I think I'm going to enjoy teaching you how to behave.'

She got her breath back, then glowered at him. 'You're despicable.'

'And you are a vision of beauty,' he pronounced solemnly. 'Especially when you're aroused.' He placed his forefinger under her chin and tilted her head upwards until she was forced to submit to his gaze. 'Your skin goes a delicate shade of pink and those blue eyes shine with fire.' His voice became lower and huskier. 'You're a very beautiful woman, Catriona. I've never seen lips that look so kissable and tempting as yours.'

A memory stirred and an alarm bell rang in her head. She pushed his hand away and snorted with derision. 'That must be one of your standard lines, is it? You used it on me in London. But I suppose that a libertine like you with so many women in his past is bound to get his wires crossed now and again.'

'No...' he explained, unabashed. 'I was curious to find out just how good your memory was of that night in London.' He took her arm again and said pleasantly, 'Now, let's have that stroll along the riverbank and we'll discover what else you remember.'

She was glad to get off the terrace. There were too many curious glances being cast their way for comfort. 'You can let go my arm,' she said quietly. 'It's not as if there's any place I can run to, is there?'

Although the sun had dipped lower in the sky the evening was comfortably warm, and the still air was filled with that intoxicating perfume which was particular to the Western Highlands. The broad, fast-flowing river gurgled and cavorted over and around its boulder-strewn course, pausing to rest occasionally in deep, dark brown pools.

The grass was soft and springy underfoot as they strolled slowly upstream and she kept a good arm's length away in case he suddenly took it in his mind to grab her again and do the deed there and then. She wouldn't be surprised at anything he did from now on.

They walked in silence for a few hundred yards then suddenly, beneath the dark green canopy of a huge Scots pine, he stopped and slowly surveyed the scene. She backed away and eyed him with caution.. She knew it! His over-active hormones were on the warpath and he couldn't wait until tonight.

At last his grey eyes came to rest on her and she took a deep breath. 'Why are you looking at me like that?' she demanded with a betraying tremble.

'Like what?'

The puzzled frown on his face didn't fool her for one minute. 'You know like what,' she wavered. 'It's all you think about, isn't it? You've got a one-track mind.'

His eyes flickered in amusement and the frown changed into a sardonic grin as understanding dawned. 'It seems to me that you're the one with the one-track mind,' he drawled. 'First of all you tempt me in the shower and now you're at it again, outside and in full view of anyone who happens to pass by! You're a very promiscuous young lady, Catriona McNeil. I'm sure your mother would be shocked if she knew.' He gave a sad, reluctant shake of his head, then sighed. 'Again I'll have to forego the pleasure on the grounds of safety. If we indulge ourselves here I'd be up all night picking pine needles from your tender little posterior.'

Her mouth sagged open. Oh, why couldn't the ground just open up and swallow her? If it really was his intention to make a fool of her then she was making it very easy for him.

Gathering what shreds of dignity she had left, she faced him calmly. 'If I misinterpreted your reason for stopping at this spot then it's your own fault. I don't think there's a woman in the world who would feel safe in your company.'

'Some women like it that way,' he remarked glibly. 'In fact, most do. The least it does is let them know that they have the ability to attract a man. Why else do they wear perfume, make-up and pretty clothes?'

She knew there was an answer to that typically male chauvinist argument. It was just a pity that she couldn't think of it at the moment. Instead she had to be content with saying sharply, 'Well, I'm not one of them.'

He laughed sourly. 'Then why did you turn up at our first date looking as if you'd just stepped from the pages of a fashion magazine?'

She frowned. 'How was I supposed to turn up? It was a dinner date at a West End restaurant, wasn't it? I'd have looked out of place in baggy sweater and jeans, wouldn't I? And don't tell me you wouldn't have cared.' She tossed the hair out of her eyes. 'You had invited me to dinner and I was simply paying you the compliment of dressing suitably for the occasion.'

His eyes turned hard and he gave a grunt of derisory scepticism before turning his back on her and continuing with his stroll.

She stared after him indignantly, then caught up with him and blocked his path. With her legs apart and her hands on her hips she stuck her chin out and demanded hotly, 'If you've got some kind of accusation to make then make it instead of just walking away. I'm not a mind-reader.'

He looked her up and down, which only infuriated her further, then he frowned. 'Are you having another tantrum? You know what happened the last time.'

She took a nervous step backwards. 'I'm not having a tantrum. I just want to know what was so wrong about the way I was dressed. You seemed to like it at the time. Or was that another one of your lies?'

'Oh, it was no lie. In fact you looked positively dazzling,' he admitted readily. 'But of course I didn't really know who you were at the time, did I, Miss McNeil?'

Her blue eyes were perplexed. 'What does that have to do it? You knew my name and where I lived, didn't you? Wasn't that enough?'

'It was a designer dress in silk, as I recall,' he mused aloud. 'It must have cost a fortune. And you didn't wear it just to pay me a compliment, as you suggest. It was obviously chosen to make you look even more attractive than you are.'

She was beginning to get a bad feeling about this. He was leading up to something.

'Where did you get it, by the way?' he asked. 'I suppose you borrowed it from the shop you work in?'

Her hands dropped to her side as embarrassment took over from indignation. 'It…it was reject stock,' she muttered, then added, as if it was some feeble excuse, 'There was a flaw in the hem.'

'I see…' He was regarding her now with scornful amusement. 'You didn't tell me that at the time though, did you? I also recall that when I complimented you on the dress you said…' He scratched at his ear thoughtfully, trying to remember her exact words. 'Yes…you said that you'd had a problem deciding what to wear and that you'd only made up your mind at the last minute. Now that's not the kind of thing a woman would say unless she's trying to give the impression that she's got a wardrobe full of the damn things, is it?'

She swallowed, then blustered, 'All right! But it was only a dress, dammit! I don't know what you're making all the fuss about.' She looked at him reproachfully. 'I may have told a little white lie but it's nothing compared to what you did to me.'

He shrugged. 'As I told you before, you only have yourself to blame for that.' Her mouth opened in protest but he gave her a warning look, then growled in exasperation, 'I know you're not a fool, Catriona. Why can't you see that you engineered your own downfall? If you hadn't tried to pretend that you were something you're not then things might have been different between us.'

She stared at him in bewilderment, then shook her head in despair. 'I'm sorry. I haven't a clue what you're talking about. You'll have to explain it to me.'

He gestured her to follow him with a flick of his head and they resumed their stroll along the riverbank. The sun was lower now, getting ready to bed down behind the mountains in the west where the sky was turning a fiery red.

'The dress was the least of it,' he explained quietly. 'But, taken together with all the other things you said or didn't say, you created an image of yourself that was far from the truth.' He laughed at a sudden memory. 'You were so convincing that when I arrived in Kindarroch I was naive enough to ask directions to the McNeil estate. Naturally enough no one had ever heard of it. And the only Catriona McNeil they knew was your good self, so they pointed me in the direction of your parents' house. It was only then that I realised how you'd fooled me.'

She had the grace to blush. Everything he said was true. There were more ways of lying than by using the spoken word. If someone assumed something about you and you did nothing about it then that was as good as lying, wasn't it? Just as she'd let him go on believing that the luxury flat in Palmerston Court belonged to her instead of telling him that she was merely a lodger.

Suddenly he turned, grabbed her by the shoulders and gave her a good shake. 'Why did you do it?' He shook her again, making her teeth chatter. 'Give me one good reason for acting so foolishly.'

She broke free and shouted at him angrily, 'Because I wanted to impress you. Yes, you're right. I wanted to attract your attention. I couldn't believe that a man like you could possibly be interested in someone like me. I was trying to be smart and sophisticated, like the women who come into the shop.' She bit her lip and looked away. 'I hope you're satisfied now. I wanted you to love me but all I got was one humiliation after another. Now why don't you do the world a favour? Tie a rock to your neck and go and jump in the river.'

He began to laugh. At first it was a quiet chuckle, as if he was finding the whole thing strangely amusing, but it grew in strength until to her ears it became more like a sound of brutal derision, and her heart felt heavy with despair. She'd just unburdened her soul to him…and he thought it was funny! With a final look of disgust she left him standing there and retraced her steps wearily towards the hotel.

After a moment he caught up with her and walked alongside.

'Give me your hand, Catriona,' he said, reaching for it.

She shrugged him off and muttered, 'Leave me alone. I hate you.'

'You're being very childish about this,' he remarked.

She didn't even bother responding to that and she quickened her pace, her eyes misting over.

When they reached the hotel foyer he tried to steer her towards the cocktail bar but she held back. 'No, thanks, I'm tired and I'm going up to the room.'

His grip on her arm tightened and he growled, 'I still have things to discuss.'

'Not with me, you haven't,' she replied with an adamant shake of her head. 'And the only discussion I'm going to have is with myself, and I need peace and quiet for that.' She pulled herself free from his grip and headed for the lift.

CHAPTER NINE

THE room was in darkness. For the last fifteen minutes Catriona had stood unmoving at the window, watching sadly as the deepening purple of the sky revealed the stars one by one. She ignored the gentle creaking sound of the door opening, and the soft light as it intruded briefly from the corridor outside. The door closed again. There was the sound of a tray being placed on the table then the click of a switch as the shaded light came on.

'I've brought wine and some cold chicken sandwiches in case we feel like a late-night snack,' Ryan said. 'I thought it would save Room Service the trouble.'

She continued staring out of the window, unwilling to confront him again and get involved in another slanging match—although she knew it was unavoidable sooner or later. 'You needn't have bothered,' she said tiredly. 'I'm not hungry.'

'Nor particularly friendly-sounding, either,' he observed, to the accompaniment of a cork being drawn. 'Never mind. A couple of glasses of wine will put that right.'

There he went again, with his arrogant assumption that all he had to do was snap his fingers to bring her to heel, she thought bitterly. Well, no longer. She should never have let him get the whip hand from the beginning. But it wasn't too late. She was tired of dancing to his tune and now she'd had her fill of it.

She turned slowly, her face at once resigned yet determined. 'You can have the bed if you like. I'll sleep on the settee. I'd much rather move to another room but I don't want to put the hotel staff to any unnecessary trouble.'

He studied her impassively, then shrugged. 'Forget the staff. That's why they work here. It can be arranged easily enough. I'll phone Reception right now if that's what you really want. They'll be only too pleased to rent out another room.' He poured wine into a couple of glasses and handed her one. 'So you think that my threats are all a bluff, do you?'

She took the offered glass and eyed him defiantly. 'They may or may not be, but I'm past caring. When I get back to Kindarroch tomorrow I'm going to do what I should have done as soon as you turned up. I'm going to tell the truth. I'll tell everyone how I was foolish enough to go to bed with you on our very first date.' She bit her lip. 'That'll hurt my parents but it can't be helped. After that I'm going to tell them how I tried to get my own back when you deserted me and how you then came here to blackmail me.'

He pursed his lips thoughtfully, then nodded. 'That is one way out of your predicament. I mean, they're more likely to believe one of their own than take the word of an outsider like me.'

She could see that amused gleam in his eyes again, as if he was silently jeering at her, and she retorted coldly, 'They're more likely to believe the truth, you mean.'

'You'd be surprised at how blind some people can be to the truth, Catriona,' he said with irony. 'Even yourself. You find it easier to judge a person by their reputation than by personal experience.'

She gave a bitter snort, 'Well, I've had personal experience of you, and you certainly lived up to your reputation. My biggest regret is that they came in the wrong order.' She walked stiffly past him and laid her drink on the table. 'You'd better phone Room Service and have them send up a couple of spare blankets.'

He grinned. 'That won't be necessary. You're forgetting that I'm a gentleman. If you're really serious then you can have the bed and I'll have the settee.' He took a step forward and laid his hands gently on her shoulders. 'But I really don't think it'll come to that. I'm sure we can settle our differences.'

Her throat tightened and her body trembled even under the lightness of his touch. 'You…you're not going to make me change my mind, Ryan.'

His lips descended gently on hers and for a moment her head swam, before she found the strength to wrench her head aside. 'No…' she gasped. 'Let me go, damn you.'

His grip on her merely tightened and once again his mouth found hers. This time the kiss was harder…more demanding…and she fought against the temptation to yield there and then. She tried to make her mind a blank and her body unresponsive to his touch but it was like trying to ignore the scorching heat of a furnace. She could feel the thrusting strength of his desire as he crushed her against his lean, muscular body, and with her last remaining strength she managed to wriggle free.

Hot-eyed and panting for breath, she backed away from him. 'It…it's no good, Ryan. I'm not giving in. Not this time. For once I'm going to do something right in my life.'

In the light cast by the shaded lamp it was hard to

be sure of the expression on his face, but there was no trace of anger or defeat in his voice when he said quietly, 'You can't hope to win against the driving force of your own sexuality, Catriona. Are you willing to kiss me once more and put it to the test?'

Her heart was on a roller coaster ride again. One more kiss like that and it would be game, set and match to him, and they both knew it. She shook her head. 'No. P-please keep away from me.'

There was a nerve-stretching silence, then she watched dry-mouthed as he removed his jacket and tie. He wouldn't dare! Would he? A nerve in the pit of her stomach twitched as he picked up her glass from the table and thrust it at her. 'Drink this,' he ordered quietly. 'You and I are going to have a long talk.'

She accepted the glass reluctantly and muttered, 'Wine isn't going to make any difference. Neither is talking. I've already told you. My mind is made up.'

'Then perhaps I can change it, Catriona.' There was a look in his eyes she'd never seen before. Sincerity? Either that or it was just a trick of the light, she thought.

'Well, you can try if you like but you'll be wasting your time,' she vowed. 'Anyway, it's getting late and I'm tired, so say your piece and get it over with.'

'Supposing I told you that I loved you?' he demanded in a low, husky voice.

'Don't be ridiculous,' she said wearily. 'You don't know when to give up, do you?'

'What if I told you that I want to devote the rest of my life to you and you alone, Catriona?' He reached out and stroked her hair gently. 'I want us to have children and watch them grow up together. And I want us to grow old together.'

The glass in her hand trembled but her voice was firm enough. 'I wouldn't believe you.' He'd resort to anything to get her into bed, she thought. 'You surely don't think I'm going to believe anything you say, do you?'

His voice was low and determined. 'This time it's different. I've never been more serious in my life. As soon as we get back to Kindarroch tomorrow I'm going to ask your father's permission to marry you. That's how they go about things up here, isn't it? And then we'll call on the Reverend McPhee and make arrangements for the grandest wedding Kindarroch has ever seen.'

Her throat tightened and her eyes grew moist. Why was he doing this to her? she thought in despair. Didn't he realise how much he'd already hurt her? What kind of satisfaction did he derive from putting her through this emotional wringer?

With a struggle she kept her voice even. 'I'm sorry, Ryan. Even if I did believe you you'd be the last man on earth I'd want for a husband. I'm just one of those old-fashioned girls who happens to believe that a husband and wife should be faithful to one another. With the best will in the world I can't see you sticking to your marriage vows for long.' She shrugged regretfully. 'I'm not condemning you. I'll leave that to your own conscience. And if that's the way you want to live your life then go ahead. But you'll have to do it without me.'

He sighed. 'There you go again. You're judging me by my reputation.'

'Not entirely,' she reminded him grimly. 'I have

first-hand experience of your methods. I was one of your victims, remember?'

He grinned. 'And by far the most beautiful.'

'Oh, shut up!' she said angrily. 'The time has long passed for that kind of false flattery.'

'Yes…' he said, eyeing her thoughtfully. 'And the truth about my so-called reputation would be difficult for anyone to believe. But you're so convinced that I'm a liar that in your case it would be impossible. Well, I've only got myself to blame for that.' He grinned again and spread his hands. 'All I can do is throw myself on your mercy.'

'Do you mean the same kind of mercy you showed me and all the other women you used? The ones who only got what they deserved—according to you.'

'I'm making no apologies for what I did…except to you.'

The retort she was going to make died on her lips and she looked at him uncertainly. 'I hope you aren't going to insult my intelligence by putting forward some sort of excuse for your behaviour, are you? Or are you about to swear with your hand on your heart that you've suddenly seen and regretted the error of your ways?'

'No excuses. Only reasons,' he said gravely. 'All I'm asking is for you to listen and give me a chance to explain.'

She took a sip of her wine, eyeing him with scepticism over the rim of her glass. This should be good, she thought. He was going to explain away all those women he'd seduced then ditched! Of course, he'd be used to doing this. He probably kept *The Idiot's Guide To Seduction and Plausible Excuses* in his back pocket.

She took another sip, thought, What the hell—it'll be good for a laugh at least, and said, 'Go ahead, then. I'm listening.'

His eyes seemed to flicker in surprise at her answer, then he adopted a sombre look before turning and going over to the window to stare up at the night sky.

She watched him with justified cynicism. It was much easier for a person to lie when they had their back to you and their face was hidden. She didn't know why she was wasting her time.

For what seemed an interminable time he stood in silence, gazing up at the stars. Looking for inspiration, no doubt, she told herself. Some story designed to tug at her heartstrings and break her resistance. Well, it would have to be a work of art to do that.

When he did finally speak his voice was so low that she had to strain to hear. 'It was a clear, starry night just like this when I got the call from the police…' He lapsed into silence for a moment, then he seemed to square his shoulders before turning to face her. 'I'd better start from the beginning,' he said apologetically.

He could start wherever he liked, she thought. It wasn't going to make the least bit of difference to her.

'When I was twenty years old my widowed mother remarried and I acquired a stepbrother. Malcolm was only ten. A great kid. Always laughing and game for anything. We became very close…'

Catriona groaned inwardly. She remembered Madge telling her how his younger stepbrother had been killed and how Ryan had taken the blow very hard. Surely he wasn't going to play the sympathy card. But why else would he be telling her about it?

What could it possibly have to do with the present situation?

'There'd been an accident,' Ryan went on. 'Malcolm had driven at high speed into a concrete bridge support. Thankfully no one else was involved, but I couldn't understand how it had happened. In the first place Malcolm was one of the country's most promising young racing-drivers. He never drank, and according to the police there hadn't been anything mechanically wrong with the car.'

He ran a hand tiredly across his brow in the manner of one reliving a time of grief.

She broke in uncomfortably, 'Look…I'm sorry about your brother, I really am… But…'

'Just let me finish, will you?'

She backed down under the soft reprimand and bit her lip. This wasn't going quite the way she'd expected.

His voice was firmer now, with a hard edge of anger. 'The funeral was supposed to be a private affair, but a young girl managed to slip in and she sat by herself at the rear of the church. I could see that she'd been weeping and she approached me after the service saying that she knew the truth about the accident. I took her for a coffee and listened to one of the most sickening stories I've ever heard.' He paused again, and Catriona was taken aback by the look of icy anger on his face.

'It seems that Malcolm had been invited to a party in Chelsea that night,' he said bitterly. 'It was full of the usual crowd of social butterflies you always get at these occasions. You can see them any day of the week in the cafés and wine bars of Chelsea. They sit there gossiping and scheming among themselves.

Their only ambition in life is to meet and marry someone rich enough to keep them in a style they'd like to become accustomed to.'

Catriona stared at him. It was uncanny. She knew exactly the kind of women he was describing. Hadn't two of them been sitting at the next table that day when Madge had taken her to lunch?

She was all ears now as Ryan went on. 'According to this girl, Malcolm had rebuffed a couple of them when their overtures became too embarrassing, so they decided to teach him a lesson. While he was up dancing they spiked his drink with a drug. Wouldn't it be *fun*, they thought, if the handsome and ambitious young racing-driver crashed and lost his driving licence?'

Catriona was appalled and she gave an involuntary gasp. 'That…that's diabolical!'

Ryan nodded bitterly. 'Yeah…that's what I thought. I don't suppose it even entered their stupid heads that they were putting his life at risk.'

'The girl who told you this? Was she one of them?'

'She swore she wasn't. And I believed her. She'd known what was going on, though, and her conscience was tearing her apart. I never did find out who actually tampered with his drink, but as far as I was concerned they were all responsible. What I did get from the girl, though, was a list of the names of the most likely women, who regularly got their kicks at these kind of parties.'

If she hadn't been so overwhelmed by the story Catriona would have been able to deduce what was coming next, but she could only stare at him numbly when he remarked, 'The McNeils aren't the only ones prepared to avenge an injury, Catriona. That's what I meant when I said that you and I are alike in many ways. Those women had used my brother for their own amusement so I decided to use them.'

She still didn't get it. 'You mean…by sleeping with them?'

He shrugged. 'What else? They had no idea that Malcolm was my stepbrother. I was—to quote the title the tabloids gave me—''London's most eligible bachelor.'' And, oh boy, if only they could get my ring on their finger they'd be rich and idle for the rest of their lives. You could almost see their mouths watering at the prospect. So I led them on…took what I wanted, then moved on to the next one.' He shrugged again. 'It was my way of humiliating them. Considering what they'd done to Malcolm they got off lightly.' He paused and looked at her questioningly. 'But I don't suppose you approve.'

She was trying to think of an answer to that when the horrifying truth sneaked up and hit her like ton of bricks. She swallowed hard and her eyes widened. 'That's why you picked on me, wasn't it? You thought that I was one of…them!'

He spread his hands in a gesture of contrition. 'You weren't on the list, but you were so convincing in the part. You've already admitted that you tried to emulate them because you thought in your innocence that I would be attracted by that type. You even led me to believe that you were a regular Chelsea partygoer.'

She sat down on the edge of the bed as her head began to spin. No one could make up a story like that on the spur of the moment. And it certainly had the ring of truth. He was right. She had engineered her own destruction.

'All right…' she said slowly, looking up at him

suspiciously. 'I believe that part of it. But what about the rest? You never loved me then and you couldn't have loved me when you came up here with your threats of blackmail. What about all the pictures of me you brought up? The ones in your suitcase. The pictures you're going to show everyone unless I do what you want?'

'An empty threat,' he admitted wryly. 'A bluff. There was only one and you tossed it in the harbour, remember? You can put your mind at rest by searching my luggage when we get back to Kindarroch.'

'I will,' she promised. 'You can bet your life on it.' She kept staring up at him warily, her heart desperate to believe him but her mind still confused. 'So you lied to me about that,' she pointed out. 'How do I know you're not lying now when you say that you love me?'

He spread his hands in appeal and said quietly, 'You'll just have to take my word for it, Catriona. It's your decision.'

'Huh!' She shook her head in frustration. 'You've got a funny way of treating someone you claim to love. Have you any idea of the heartache and worry you've caused me? No one does that to someone they love.'

He stepped towards her and pulled her gently to her feet. After kissing her tenderly on the forehead he gazed into her troubled eyes and explained, 'When I first arrived here I expected to meet the rich, spoilt brat I'd met in London, and I was going to get my own back on her for pulling that Trixie Trotter stunt.' He cupped her face in his hands and kissed her lightly on the mouth before continuing, 'Instead, I met you. And you were like a breath of sweet air after the sickening hypocrisy of the women I'd been involving myself with. I couldn't do anything other than fall hopelessly in love with you.'

Her eyes searched his face desperately and her heart was almost in her mouth. 'If…if that's true why didn't you tell me there and then, instead of…of tormenting me the way you did?'

He gave a sigh of self-disgust, then nodded. 'Yes…that was wrong of me. But you were so antagonistic towards me in your parents' house that I decided to play the villain you believed me to be for a while. I thought you'd see through it and then we could have a good laugh and make up. But I misjudged the depth of your antagonism and things started to get out of hand. Then every time I tried to patch things up and tell you the truth you beat me to it with a tongue lashing. I should have put my hand over your pretty little mouth and yelled it in your ear.'

Her legs were starting to tremble again and she swallowed painfully. 'Ryan…Do you really want to marry me?'

Once more he kissed her gently on the lips, then he nuzzled her ear and whispered, 'More than anything in this world or the next, darling. I never realised how empty my life has been until now. I told you, darling. We'll start making the arrangements as soon as we get back.'

She stiffened slightly as his hands slid under her blouse. Oh God! She yearned to believe him, but dared she? In how many other ears had he whispered those very same words? His hands slid round to cup and caress both her breasts. She would have to make up her mind before it was too late. Her defences were

already crumbling under his sweet and tempting on-
slaught.

She made an effort to protest, but his mouth descended once more on her parted lips and the hot rush
of blood pounded in her ears. His fingers deftly undid
the clasp on her bra and she shivered with sensual
delight as his hands roved over the curves and con-
tours of her body. She could feel the strong beat of
his heart against her own, and the clean, masculine
smell of him heightened and inflamed her senses. His
fingers rapidly undid the front of her blouse, and as
it fell open he lowered his head and closed his lips
gently around one of her nipples.

She arched back, a soft moan escaping from her
lips at the almost unbearable pleasure as his teeth bit
gently, and her hands went to his head, her fingers
clutching and entwining themselves in his dark hair.
She was dimly aware of her trousers being unzipped
and sliding down over her slim hips, then his right
hand set her skin on fire as it travelled gently over
her stomach and inserted itself beneath the top of her
briefs.

'God! You're beautiful, darling,' he whispered in
her ear. 'No woman has ever made me feel this way
before.'

His words cut through the haze of sensual pleasure
and stirred a memory. She tried to dismiss it. Nothing
was going to spoil this moment. But the memory was
like a troublesome itch that wouldn't go away, and
then suddenly it came all too sharply into focus.
Those were the exact words he'd said to her that night
in London!

With a sickening rush her doubts about him came
back to torture her mind. The words had been an

empty, hollow mockery then. How could she be sure they weren't equally meaningless now? Was she simply being over-cautious and sensitive, or was she about to repeat the biggest mistake she'd ever made in her life? Her mind was in a fever as his hands continued their intimate exploration and she bit down hard on her lip. There was one way to find out. It was going to take every ounce of her willpower but she had to know the truth. If he deceived her again she'd never, ever get over it.

She eased herself as gently as she could out of his arms and took a step backwards. Painfully aware of her state of near nudity, she pulled her briefs back up over her hips then sat on the edge of the bed and looked up at him in embarrassment. 'I…I'm sorry, Ryan. I don't want it to go any further. Not tonight.' Her voice was subdued with regret.

The desire was glistening in his eyes as he frowned and said thickly, 'What's wrong? I know you want me as much as I want you.'

She swallowed painfully. 'There's nothing wrong. It's just that I…I…' Her voice faltered. 'You're right. I want to. Believe me, darling, I really want you. But I…I can't. Not yet.'

He knelt beside her, took her hand in his and studied her with genuine concern. 'You're not feeling ill, are you?'

She shook her head. 'No. It's nothing like that.'

He gave her hand a gentle squeeze. 'Then tell me.'

'You…you wouldn't understand. You'd just tell me that I was being silly and childish.'

Frowning again he said, 'Why don't you let me decide that?'

She bit her lip again, then took a deep breath.

'When we made love in London…it was the first time for me. I…I've always felt guilty about that. I'd always promised myself that—no, don't apologise, darling—I'd always vowed to keep myself for my husband on our wedding night.' She looked at him imploringly. 'I know it sounds crazy but I feel I could somehow ease my conscience if…if I could find the strength this time to wait…until our wedding night.'

She lowered her eyes demurely. For a moment he said nothing, then he got to his feet and she looked up slowly to measure his reaction. There was frustration in the tense lines on his face, but that was only to be expected. He wasn't the only one to feel that way, although in her own case it was self-inflicted. There was no anger, though. Nor the hint of any intention to achieve his aim by a further attack on her teetering defences.

'I…I'm sorry, darling,' she murmured. 'Do you think I'm being silly?'

He seemed to tower over her, and for a moment his eyes held a look of hungry disappointment, then, incredibly, he gave a rueful smile. 'I think you're just being you, Catriona. The most wonderful girl God ever created.' He held out his hand to help her to her feet. 'Now go and brush your teeth while I steal one of your blankets.'

The room was filled with bright moonlight and Catriona hadn't slept a wink in the last two hours. Judging by the restless sounds coming from the settee, it was the same with Ryan. She'd gone over his story time and time again in her head, searching for inconsistencies…any hint that the whole thing was nothing more than an elaborate deception…but everything seemed to fit.

There was only one niggling doubt, and that concerned his claim that whenever he'd previously tried to tell her the truth she hadn't even been prepared to listen. She'd been antagonistic towards him right from the start. Well, there might be a lot of truth in that. Anyway, surely by now he deserved the benefit of the doubt.

She lay for another half-hour. Tomorrow she would know for certain. She closed her eyes but it was no use. No, dammit! She knew for certain now. Propping herself up on one elbow, she called softly, 'Ryan…are you awake?'

There was a short silence, then, 'Yes.'

She bit her lip, then lay down again and stared up at the ceiling. 'I'm sorry about…about that night in Cardini's.'

For a moment there was no reply, then she heard him chuckle softly. 'Forget it.'

'I…I can't. Your business reputation…I had no right to…to ruin it the way I did.'

'You didn't,' he said quietly. 'I contacted the paper the following morning and explained that 'Trixie Trotter' was an employee I'd had to sack recently for dishonesty and who obviously had a grudge against me. Of course I was too much of a gentleman to mention any names. The editor was kind enough to print my statement in the next edition.'

Catriona's first reaction to his confession was anger. He'd used a lie to justify his threats. Then she thought about it and held her tongue. After all, if the paper hadn't published his excuse she might well have caused him a lot of undeserved bad publicity.

Another thought occurred to her and she said quietly, 'If your reputation is still intact then there's nothing to stop you going back to resume your life in London, is there?'

'Nothing in the world, Catriona,' he agreed softly. 'Except that I'd much rather spend the rest of my life here with you.'

She lay staring into the darkness for a few minutes more, then she murmured, 'Ryan...?'

'I'm still awake.'

'I'm feeling cold, darling, and so must you be. I think it would be more sensible if you brought your blanket over here, then we could both keep warm.'

At first it didn't look as if he was going to respond, and she held her breath. She wouldn't be able to look him in the eye in the morning if he turned her down now. Had she made one more of her embarrassing mistakes?

At last she heard the creak of the settee and she saw him rise and walk towards her. Naked in the soft moonlight, he made a magnificent figure, and she pushed the blankets aside and opened her arms in welcome.

He lay down beside her and as their bodies entwined he whispered softly, 'You will never, ever feel cold again, my darling. That's a promise.'

CHAPTER TEN

THE entire population of Kindarroch had been at the wedding, either crammed into the tiny church or waiting outside to cheer and shower the bride and groom with confetti as they emerged.

Now the traditional *ceilidh* was in full swing in the large lounge of the Harbour Hotel. The dancing and the wild Highland music would go on until the wee small hours of the following morning, or even later if the supply of whisky held out, but Ryan and Catriona would be well on their way to their honeymoon by then. A month of sheer bliss on a secluded island in the Caribbean.

For the moment Catriona had retired to a quiet corner after a particularly energetic reel, and she was content just to sip her drink and watch the crowd enjoying themselves. She'd changed from her wedding gown into a flared skirt and cool cotton blouse. Then a voice at her side said, 'Hello there, Mrs Hind. So this is where you're hiding yourself.'

She smiled at Ryan. How wonderful he looked, she told herself again...the handsomest man in the room. No...not just the room...the whole planet...the universe, even! Her heart was filled with pride. 'I've been up for the last six dances,' she explained with a smile. 'My feet are demanding a ten-minute break or they're going to go on strike.'

Ryan grinned. 'I never expected such a crowd. You're a very popular woman in these parts, Mrs

Hind. Everyone keeps telling me how lucky a man I am to get you as my wife. Not that I need telling.'

'And you're a very popular man, Mr Hind,' she said. She reached up and gave him a resounding kiss. 'Especially with me. Have you any idea how deliriously happy you've made me? Have you any idea at all?'

'No.' His grey eyes gleamed with good humour. 'Would you like to whisper it in my ear?'

'I would. But it would take the rest of the night. And I'd end up chewing your earlobe, it looks so delicious.' She saw the infinite tenderness in his eyes as he smiled at her, and this time the lump in her throat was there for all the right reasons. But wouldn't it be terrible if she started to cry now and spoiled everything? she thought. Smiling back at him, she murmured, 'Anyway, there are better ways to show it than by talking. You're going to find that out as soon as we're alone.'

His arms went around her waist and he playfully kissed the tip of her nose. 'That sounds interesting. I can hardly wait. Body language is always more reliable than the spoken word.' He was about to kiss her again when Madge elbowed her way through the crowd and confronted them.

'Are you two love-birds going to stand there gazing into each others eyes like a pair of soppy kids for the rest of the night?' She playfully prodded Ryan in the chest with her finger and said, 'I've been trying to get a dance with you for the last hour, but someone always beats me to it.' Then, with a look of irrepressible devilment, she immediately took possession of his arm and began dragging him back to the dance floor. Throwing Catriona a sweetly reproving smile, she said, 'Don't worry. I'm not going to kidnap him and hold him to ransom. I just want to borrow him for five minutes. You'll have him for the rest of your life, you lucky thing, you.'

Catriona laughed at the look of helpless apology on Ryan's face before they were swallowed up by the crowd of dancers, then she sipped at her drink again, remembering Madge's reaction when she'd told her the news over the phone three days ago...

'You're getting married on Saturday?' Madge had repeated in astonishment. 'Well, that's absolutely wonderful. I'm delighted for you, Catriona, but it's a bit sudden, isn't it? Who on earth is the lucky man? One of your local ex-boyfriends?'

'No, Madge.' She'd hesitated for only a moment before remembering that Madge had been around long enough to take even news like this in her stride. 'It's Ryan Hind,' she said quickly.

There was a sharp intake of breath and Catriona could just picture Madge fumbling in her packet, then producing and hurriedly lighting a cigarette. She was right. There was a familiar cough, then Madge said, 'Excuse me. There must be something wrong with the connection. I could have sworn that you said "Ryan Hind," there.'

'There's nothing wrong with the phone, Madge. You heard right. Believe it or not, but we're in love and I'm the happiest girl in the world. We were both terribly wrong about him, Madge. Honestly, as soon as you get to know him you'll understand just what I mean.'

There was another bout of coughing, then something that sounded like a groan. 'Well, I suppose you know your own mind, my dear girl, but I sincerely hope you aren't making a terrible mistake. I mean, I wouldn't like to see him leaving you standing at the altar with egg on your face.'

'He won't do that, Madge,' she assured her. 'He's already bought the ring and made the arrangements at the church. All the invitations have been sent out. And after the wedding there'll be a grand *ceilidh* in the hotel.'

'A grand what?'

'A huge party. With singing and dancing and eating and drinking.'

'Oh, well, that's not so bad,' Madge said, sounding relieved. 'If he's bought the ring then that means that you can always sue him for breach of promise if he jilts you at the last moment.'

Catriona laughed. 'You're a terrible old cynic, Madge. Now, I insist that you be here for the wedding. Ryan has already made all the travel arrangements to get you here. A limousine will pick you up just after lunch on Friday, you'll stay overnight in a five-star hotel in Edinburgh, and if you leave just after breakfast the next morning you should be up here in plenty of time for the ceremony. Please tell me you'll come.'

Madge laughed dryly. 'Are you joking? To watch the Golden Hind striking his colours and being brought into harbour by a slip of a girl? Of course I'll come. My dear girl, I wouldn't miss it for the world!'

Well, Madge had arrived today with time to spare, and had immediately demanded an explanation for this sudden change of heart. She had taken a lot of convincing, but finally seemed satisfied that Catriona hadn't lost her marbles and that Ryan wasn't keeping his car engine warmed up for a fast getaway.

After that it had been time to introduce Madge to her parents, and Catriona would have been lying to herself if she hadn't admitted that that had been a daunting prospect. But she needn't have worried. She should have had more faith in Madge, who had immediately sized up the situation and had magically transformed herself into everyone's favourite maiden aunt. She'd even refrained from smoking in their presence, and her mother had taken to her straight away.

'She's a really charming lady,' her mother had said when she'd got the first chance to confide in Catriona. 'Very genteel and gracious. You can tell that she comes from a good family. Good breeding always tells, doesn't it? I've already told her how grateful I am for the way she gave you a job and looked after you in London. She really seems to think the world of you.'

Glad, and wise enough to leave it at that, she'd hugged her mother and said, 'And I think the world of you, Mum.'

Madge and Ryan were still on the dance floor, demonstrating their own interpretation of Scottish country dancing to the delight and cheers of the other guests, and Catriona spotted old Morag, sitting by herself on the other side of the room.

She made her way through the crowd and looked down fondly. 'Hello, Morag. Are you enjoying the *ceilidh*? Would you like another drink? Or maybe a wee morsel of cold chicken?'

Morag smiled up at her. 'That's very kind and thoughtful of you, Catriona.' She held out her empty glass. 'Just a small whisky and water would be fine. It's grand for putting life back into these tired old bones.'

Catriona took the glass and gave an understanding smile. 'I'll be right back.' She made her way over to the buffet: two long tables placed end to end and sagging under the weight of sides of ham, roast beef, lamb, venison, duck, smoked salmon and illegally caught grouse—to which Police Sergeant McCabe was tactfully turning a blind eye, although he wasn't averse to helping himself to a slice or two now and again, to everyone's amusement.

Donnie, who was in charge of dispensing the drinks refilled the glass and Catriona took it back to Morag, then sat down beside her. For a moment they watched the dancers whirling by, then Morag sipped at her drink and smiled. 'Your friend from London, Madge, seems to be having a good time.'

Catriona nodded in agreement. 'Aye. But that's hardly surprising when you get to know her. Madge is one of those larger than life people who could have a good time if she was stuck on a desert island with only the Reverend McPhee for company. She was very good to me when I was down in London. A real friend. She was the one who—' Suddenly she stopped in embarrassment, then gave a self-conscious laugh. 'Of course I don't need to tell you, do I? You were the one who told me before I'd even left that I'd meet someone who'd help me. You even said that it would be a woman. And you also told me that I'd meet a rich and handsome man just waiting to fall in love with me. Well, everything you told me has come true, Morag. I should never have doubted you for a moment.'

Morag regarded her fondly. 'And has Ryan come up to your expectations?'

She felt that hard lump settle in her throat again

and she nodded. 'He…he's more than I ever dared to hope for, Morag. Not even in my wildest dreams. He's the most wonderful man in the world and I'm going to love him to bits for the rest of my life.' She paused and gave a sheepish grin. 'Mind you, we had a few problems to begin with, but that's all sorted out now.'

'Aye…' said Morag quietly. 'He's a handsome-looking man, right enough, but he needs someone like you. I've a feeling that you were just made for each other. He'll be a good and kind husband.'

'I know that now,' Catriona admitted. She felt she owed Morag the whole story, but decided against it. All those stupid mistakes and misunderstandings…they were best forgotten. The future was all that mattered. A future bright with promise.

'It was nice of you to bring him up to the house for a visit yesterday,' Morag said with a quiet twinkle in her eye. 'Whose idea was it, Catriona? Yours or his?'

Now that was an odd question, she thought, giving Morag a quizzical look. 'Well…to tell the truth,' she said, feeling slightly embarrassed, 'it was his. When Ryan first saw your house up on the hill he couldn't seem to take his eyes off it. Then he asked me who lived there. I told him about you and he…he said that he wanted to meet you. I…I was reluctant to bring him at first. I thought he was only interested in buying your house because of the view. I thought he just wanted to convert it and rent it out as a holiday home.'

Morag's eyes were suddenly distant and quite unfathomable as she nodded and said quietly, 'Aye, he liked the view, right enough. And he seemed to like all my old bits and pieces of furniture. In fact he seemed quite at home, I thought.' Her eyes came alive with pleasure and she patted the back of Catriona's hand affectionately. 'Anyway, he told me that he hoped I'd live to enjoy it for many years to come and that if ever there was anything I needed I was only to let him know. Now wasn't that a very generous promise for a perfect stranger to make?'

'Ryan is a very generous man, Morag,' she said, realising more than ever now just how wrong she'd been about him at the start.

The dance came to an end and they were joined by Madge and Ryan. Madge's face was flushed and she put a hand to her brow and gasped, 'You people up here really know how to enjoy a party.' She smiled at Catriona. 'I think I'll wander over in the direction of the bar and recharge my batteries.' She gave Ryan an affectionate peck on the cheek and said, 'Now just you remember what I told you. You'd better be kind and loving to your new wife or you'll have Auntie Madge to reckon with.'

The band struck up again, but this time it was a very slow and romantic waltz. Ryan turned, seemed to hesitate, then looked at Morag and bowed gallantly. 'Morag?' he asked with grave politeness. 'Will you do me the honour of having this dance with me?'

Catriona frowned. He should have known better than to ask that! Morag was far too old and stiff to attempt dancing. She was about to come to the old woman's rescue when Morag beamed at him, put her drink aside and reached for his hand as he helped her from her seat. 'Aye…' she said softly. 'I'd like that fine.'

They were the first couple up on the floor, and suddenly everyone else seemed to be holding back. Like Catriona, they watched in wide-eyed silence. Old Morag up dancing? Surely not! Everyone knew she had arthritis and at times she could barely walk! They looked at each other with misgivings and shook their heads in wonder.

Then someone, probably Donnie the barman, dimmed the main lights and a soft overhead spotlight picked out the couple. Everyone watching held their breath as the years seemed to be magically slipping away from Morag... Her shoulders straightened and she looked somehow taller, and graceful in her movements, and it didn't take much imagination to see how beautiful she must have been as a young girl.

When the waltz ended the crowd whistled and stamped in applause as Ryan led her off the floor.

Catriona eyed her with concern as she helped her back into her seat. 'Are you feeling all right, Morag? Not dizzy or anything?'

'I'm fine. Don't worry about me,' said Morag with a strange smile of contentment. 'Your husband is a wonderful dancer, and tell me what harm any woman could come to with his strong arms to support her?' She reclaimed her drink, then chided Ryan gently, 'Now it's time you were paying more attention to your wife. I think the pair of you should slip outside for a while. The fresh air will do you good and it'll give you a chance to tell her how much you love her.'

Ryan's kiss was as warm and tender as the night itself, and Catriona nestled her head into his shoulder dreamily and murmured, 'That was a good idea of Morag's about stealing a moment to ourselves. Do you realise that this is the first time today we've had

a chance to be by ourselves?' They'd been walking
hand in hand along the beach on the south side of the
harbour, both silent and just content to be with each
other, listening to the surf whispering across the sand.
Now they had stopped to kiss and look at the stars
and talk.

'That was a really wonderful thing you did back
there,' she murmured dreamily.

He stroked her hair gently and grinned. 'It's been
a day for wonderful things. Especially putting that
ring on your finger. But which one in particular are
you talking about?'

She kissed him again. 'I'm talking about you asking
old Morag up to dance.' A tiny frown settled on her
forehead and she admitted, 'I was a bit worried at first
because...well, she's so frail that I thought it would
be too much of a strain for her. But I don't think
anyone here has ever seen her look so happy. And
now I'm glad that you thought of it.'

It was his turn to give a puzzled frown and he
tugged at his ear thoughtfully. 'It's strange you should
mention that. The truth is that I was going to ask you
to dance, and then I had this strange urge to ask
Morag instead. I just sort of felt that...that she wanted
me to. It was the damned oddest feeling I've ever had
in my life.'

She gave a dry laugh. 'Aye. Morag has that effect
on people sometimes.'

They walked on again, their hands round each
other's waists, until Ryan stopped and pointed.
'That's where our house is going to be.'

She stared excitedly across the moonlit scene.
'Where? Show me.'

Taking her by the hand, he led her up from the

beach onto a flat piece of ground covered in soft, springy grass and surrounded with silver birch and pine trees. 'Right here,' he said with a flourish. 'What do you think?'

She gazed around, then nodded. 'We used to play here when we were kids. Not the boys. Just the girls. We called it the fairies' garden. It's hidden from the road over yonder by the trees.' Giving his hand a squeeze, she murmured, 'It's perfect, darling. You couldn't have chosen a lovelier place. It'll be our private little piece of heaven on earth.'

Pleased at her reaction, he squeezed her hand in return, then said, 'They'll be making a start on the foundations tomorrow.' He took his bearings, then paced out a few steps and said, 'Now, this will be the main living room, here. With a patio overlooking a large garden. And over there will be the kitchen, with…'

'Never mind the kitchen,' she said, stopping him in mid-flow and pulling him impatiently a few more yards. 'My mind isn't on cooking at the moment. Just show me where our bedroom is going to be.'

'You're standing right in the middle of it.'

She looked down and took a little step sideways. 'Hmm… I like the carpet. And the curtains.' She walked another few paces and opened an imaginary door and exclaimed in delight, 'And this must be the *en suite* bathroom and shower. It's beautiful.'

He smiled and shook his head. 'No. That happens to be the built-in wardrobe. You want this door here.' He took a few steps to the left and opened another imaginary door.

She put her hand to her mouth. 'Silly me. Oh, yes…this is even nicer.'

'I'm pleased you like it,' he murmured. 'What do you think of the marble flooring and the pale green tiles and the gold-plated taps?'

'Gold-plated taps! My! We are extravagant, aren't we?'

'And what about the huge, sunken, whirlpool bath?'

'It takes my breath away.'

'More than enough room for both of us, you'll notice.'

She peered down at the soft grass, then looked up and smiled. 'You're definitely spoiling me.'

'I intend to. Nothing will make me happier.'

She glanced around. 'And what about the children's rooms? Where are they?'

He walked another few paces and pointed. 'One here and one over there, just by that large clump of ferns.'

She pouted in mock disappointment. 'Only two?'

'Well, they're very large rooms, as you can see. I thought, one for the boys and one for the girls.' He gave her another heated and lingering kiss, then murmured, 'Of course we can always add more rooms as the need arises.'

'Oh, well, that's all right, then,' she whispered happily. 'Will our first child be a boy or a girl?'

'Which would you prefer, darling?'

She thought for a moment, and looked up as a meteorite streaked across the sky to disappear over the western horizon. 'A boy, I think. With dark hair and lovely grey eyes just like yours. Then again, a girl would be nice too. Sometimes boys need a big sister to keep them in line.'

Another star raced across the sky and he remarked, 'Someone up there is having a party. That must be a good omen.' Taking her gently by the arm, he led her a few steps on. 'Well, here we are at the front door. And that's the driveway, leading to the road behind those trees.'

Impulsively she reached up and put her arms around his neck. 'It's wonderful, darling, and I'll make it into a home you can be proud of.'

He embraced her tightly. 'I know you will, darling.' He brushed his lips over her forehead, her eyes, her cheek, then her mouth, before murmuring, 'I'm still wondering how I was lucky enough to find a girl like you. I can't think of a single thing I've ever done to deserve you.'

'That's funny,' she sighed happily. 'I've been having the same thought about you. Perhaps it was just fate.'

'Yes. Three cheers for fate.'

'We didn't get off to a very good start, though, did we?' she reminded him nostalgically.

He grinned. 'Never mind. We'll look back on it one day and laugh. Wait until I tell our daughter of the night her mother dressed up as Trixie Trotter.'

'You wouldn't dare,' she said, giving him a poke in the ribs. 'I'd just have to tell her why I did it, and you wouldn't like that, would you?'

'Hmm... I think we'd better change the subject.' He kissed her again, long and lovingly, and she could feel the need for him quickening in her breast. He began teasing her with his tongue and she readily opened her lips. Slipping her hands beneath his jacket, she put her arms around him and pulled herself closer until their two bodies were pressed together, sending waves of loving warmth throughout her being.

His mouth left hers and he gazed down at the

moonlight shining in her hair, then very gently he laid a hand on her cheek and stroked it lightly. It was a simple gesture that told her more than mere words could do how much he loved her.

'I keep wondering if this isn't all a dream and any moment I'm going to wake up and find you gone,' he murmured. 'You're like some beautiful goddess come to life in the moonlight.'

She pressed her mouth to his and nibbled at his lip, then whispered, 'I'm no goddess. My name is Catriona Hind, the devoted wife and sole property of Mr Ryan Hind. I am his willing slave and he may do with me as he wishes, any time or any place.' She smiled and lowered her eyes demurely. 'Even here if he so desires.'

'Now that sounds like an invitation I'd be churlish to refuse,' he observed in a voice that sounded thick with sensual anticipation. 'But what about the fairies? Or don't you mind an audience?'

'Oh, the fairies in Kindarroch are very understanding about these things,' she whispered with a smile. 'Besides, they're very well bred and they'll simply pretend that we aren't here. Anyway, our honeymoon has begun so we won't be doing anything to be ashamed of, will we?'

'Oh, well, in that case...' She arched her back as he kissed her neck and began unbuttoning her blouse. Suddenly he paused and grinned. 'Do you realise that we're standing in the front hall of the house? Shouldn't we be doing this in the bedroom?'

She sighed dreamily. 'Then you'd better carry me there, darling. I'm feeling very fragile.'

Effortlessly he lifted her and cradled her in his arms. He was as mad as she was, she thought.

Gloriously, wonderfully mad. If this was what love did to you then may it last for ever. She clung to him and gazed into his eyes as he carried her the few steps then lowered her gently onto the soft grass.

There under the stars they made love. A love that somehow seemed to go beyond mere physical gratification. The feel of his hands on her naked flesh as they caressed and fondled...the sweet tremors throughout her body as his lips sought and suckled and fed on her own desire...the throbbing power of his manhood as her hand gently guided him into the sweet, moist warmth of herself...the feeling of breathless anticipation as he slowly but surely carried her higher and higher on a relentless tidal wave of unbearable ecstasy...and the shattering climax of release which left them both clinging to each other, gasping for breath.

For sweet, exhausted minutes they lay there, the sound of their beating hearts replaced by the soothing lap of the waves from the beach. Then he kissed her again, so sweetly and tenderly that she felt like crying with a happiness so intense it almost hurt.

'Do you want to go back now?' he asked softly.

'No, darling. Not yet.' She wanted to stay here like this for ever.

'Good. Neither do I.' He kissed her again softly then rolled onto his back and gazed up at the sky. 'Why couldn't we have met years ago? I'll never forget this night as long as I live.'

She propped herself on her left elbow and ran her fingertips over the smooth skin of his chest. 'I know you won't. I'll make sure of it,' she warned him with a lazy smile. 'And in any case, "years ago" I was just a spotty-faced schoolgirl you wouldn't have both-

ered looking at.' Her fingers moved playfully down-
wards to his stomach.

He reached up for her and pulled her down until
he could kiss her on the breast making her shiver with
pleasure. Gently she curled her bottom lip between
her teeth and bit down softly as his lips closed around
her nipple.

After a moment she sat up, but she still couldn't
take her eyes off him. How beautiful he looked,
stretched out below her. Long and clean limbed like
some Greek god in repose in the moonlight. It was
strange to think that he was the first man she'd ever
really known. She'd never even had a proper kiss until
she'd met him, and yet she knew in her heart that she
could never have felt like this over anyone else. Nor
would she ever for as long as she lived.

It couldn't just be put down to luck that of all the
men in the world she might have met he was the one
who'd been there at the right time in the right place.
Mere chance? Perhaps. Or then again perhaps it had
been ordained in the stars right from the beginning.

Putting that thought aside, she lay down beside him
again and rested her head on his chest. She closed her
eyes and listened to the comforting and hypnotic beat
of his heart.

No breath of wind stirred the warm blanket of the
night, and her mind slipped in and out of that state of
sweet drowsiness felt only by lovers in each other's
arms.

It might have been minutes or an hour later when
she felt him take her hand and lay it gently on his
manhood. She could feel the pulse as it began to en-
large, then she opened her eyes and stared into his

mischievously. 'Again?' she murmured in happy surprise.

'Too soon for you?' he asked with a lazy smile. 'If you're too tired we can wait till later. We've a whole lifetime ahead of us.'

She held onto him with her right hand and gave a gentle squeeze, then sat up and looked down at him. Suppressing the urge to giggle, she said in a voice of concern, 'Oh, you poor man—that must be terribly awkward. I mean, how are you going to get dressed in that condition? We can't go back to the hotel with you looking like that, can we? People are bound to notice.'

He propped himself up on his elbows and rebuked himself with a grin. 'That's the trouble with having a beautiful, sexy redhead for a wife. I suppose I'll just have to learn to keep it under better control.'

She put her finger on her chin and murmured thoughtfully, 'That might not be such a good idea, darling. The last thing I want to do is to spoil your enjoyment. Anyway, if I'm to blame then I suppose it's only right and proper that I do something about it.'

He grinned up at her. 'I like your attitude. An understanding wife is the most treasured possession a man can have. I can see that our married life is going to be a tremendous success.'

He made to sit up, but she placed the palm of her hand on his chest and firmly pushed him down. 'You've been doing all the work, darling. It's only fair that I do my share.' Slowly she moved until she was sitting astride him, then gently she guided him home and gazed down lovingly into his eyes.

Overhead the stars smiled down at them, and the

sound of the sea caressing the beach was joined by the sweet, ecstatic sighs of two lovers in the night.

Morag had slipped away quietly without telling anyone, and now she sat on her seat by the fire with a cup of hot, sweet tea in her hand and a smile of contentment on her face. Her task was over.

When the sea had claimed Seumus only his physical presence had been taken from her. His love had remained because love never died. And neither did the spirit. It awaited its rebirth and the start of a new life in the physical world. This was the wisdom she had because of her 'gift'.

It was this gift which had sent her the vision of the crowded church and the tiny child being baptised in the name of Ryan Hind. That had been over thirty years ago, and over the years she'd 'watched' the child grow to manhood. He was strong and courageous, and, like Seumus, he was a man capable of deep love and loyalty. But she'd also sensed tragedy and bitterness in his life. He'd been looking for the one woman who was capable of returning the love and respect he had to offer but it had seemed like an impossible dream.

Catriona was such a girl. Catriona had a spirit and strength to match his own and she too was capable of infinite love and tenderness. It was as if they had been fashioned for each other.

Well, Morag had succeeded in bringing them together and now they were man and wife. Oh, Ryan would be a wonderful husband, just as Seumus would have been. He would cherish Catriona all his life.

She sipped her tea and wandered over to the window. She stared dreamily out into the night. For too brief a time, at the *ceilidh*, when Ryan had 'asked' her to dance, she had been a young girl again in the arms of her husband.

She was coming to the end of her time now, but she knew that she'd live long enough to see Ryan and Catriona's first child. It would be a boy with dark hair and blue eyes. And his name would be Seumus.

MILLS & BOON®

Next Month's Romances

$\heartsuit$

Each month you can choose from a wide variety of romance novels from Mills & Boon®. Below are the new titles to look out for next month from the Presents™ and Enchanted™ series.

Presents™

JOINED BY MARRIAGE	Carole Mortimer
THE MARRIAGE SURRENDER	Michelle Reid
FORBIDDEN PLEASURE	Robyn Donald
IN BED WITH A STRANGER	Lindsay Armstrong
A HUSBAND'S PRICE	Diana Hamilton
GIRL TROUBLE	Sandra Field
DANTE'S TWINS	Catherine Spencer
SUMMER SEDUCTION	Daphne Clair

Enchanted™

NANNY BY CHANCE	Betty Neels
GABRIEL'S MISSION	Margaret Way
THE TWENTY-FOUR-HOUR BRIDE	Day Leclaire
THE DADDY TRAP	Leigh Michaels
BIRTHDAY BRIDE	Jessica Hart
THE PRINCESS AND THE PLAYBOY	Valerie Parv
WANTED: PERFECT PARTNER	Debbie Macomber
SHOWDOWN!	Ruth Jean Dale

On sale from 13th July 1998

H1 9806

**Available at most branches of
WH Smith, John Menzies, Martins, Tesco,
Asda, Volume One, Sainsbury and Safeway**

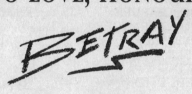

COLLECTOR'S EDITION

The *Penny Jordan Collector's Edition* is
a selection of her most popular stories,
published in beautifully designed volumes
for you to collect and cherish.

*Available from Tesco, Asda, WH Smith, John Menzies,
Martins and all good paperback stockists, at £3.10 each -
or the special price of £2.80 if you use the coupon below.
On sale from 1st June 1998.*

Valid only in the UK & Eire against purchases made in retail outlets and not in
conjunction with any Reader Service or other offer.

30ᵖ OFF
COUPON
VALID UNTIL: 31.8.1998
PENNY JORDAN COLLECTOR'S EDITION

To the Customer: This coupon can be used in part payment for a
copy of PENNY JORDAN COLLECTOR'S EDITION. Only one
coupon can be used against each copy purchased. Valid only in the
UK & Eire against purchases made in retail outlets and not in
conjunction with any Reader Service or other offer. Please do not
attempt to redeem this coupon against any other product as refusal
to accept may cause embarrassment and delay at the checkout.

To the Retailer: Harlequin Mills & Boon will redeem this coupon at
face value provided only that it has been taken in part payment for
any book in the PENNY JORDAN COLLECTOR'S EDITION. The
company reserves the right to refuse payment against misredeemed
coupons. Please submit coupons to: Harlequin Mills & Boon Ltd.
NCH Dept 730, Corby, Northants NN17 1NN.

9 904170 250306 >

0472 01316